BLAME IT ON

SOCRATES

JACK RYAN

WOODBRIDGE
PUBLISHERS

276 5th Avenue Suite 704 #944
New York, NY 10001

ISBN (Paperback): 978-1-917760-32-4
ISBN (Hardback): 978-1-917760-33-1
ISBN (eBook): 978-1-917760-34-8

To the "B-103" Crew...

TABLE OF CONTENTS

1

9:00 A.M. PHILOSOPHY

"The unexamined life is not worth living."
—Socrates

It isn't every day that your life is undone by the likes of an ancient Greek philosopher, a stray dog by the same name, and a missing letter from a long-lost lover. Trust me when I say that I could not, or would not, make this stuff up. Such is the life of a college professor.

Even when I'm in a funk, it's hard to ignore the beauty unfolding before me on campus. The quad is in full bloom with October leaves, painted in shades of gold and crimson, occupied by a sea of happy-go-lucky undergrads. Not only am I captivated by what I see, I'm also enjoying the brushing of leaves being kicked about on the sidewalk. The fall season has a sound to it. As I scurry to get to class on time, the crisp autumn air holds me hostage. I would rather stop and gather myself on a bench than teach my 9:00 a.m. class. Try as I may, I'm hard-pressed to push recent troubles out of my mind, or better yet, behind me. I mutter to myself, "What is going on? Why me? Who is to blame?"

I depend on my daily strolls cross campus to put my mind at ease. For twenty years, I've been teaching philosophy and physics at a small midwestern liberal arts college. An unusual combination, to be certain, but I'd always found it refreshing to teach two different subjects, one full of absolutes and finite numbers, the other full of unending pursuits down rabbit holes with no road map or flashlight.

My family and friends, once they moved on from being bewildered by my career choice, would surrender to the notion that my professional and private life would be dominated by reading countless books filled with abstract theories and dictums spouted off by guys in bedsheets with names too difficult to spell or pronounce.

"Patrick, here's the deal," my father said on the day I told him my plan. "I'll pay for the physics if you pay for the philosophy."

Three decades later, having taken on the necessary student loans and acquired the dishpan hands at greasy-spoon restaurants and ill-lit smoky bars, there I was, with two bachelor's degrees in usually disparate fields and a master's degree to boot, coupled with the distinction of being ABD. Consider me a paper-plate guy for life. But, to learn as much as I did about both the physical and existential natures of the universe, it was worth it.

There are many elements of student life at Simpson College to which I can relate. However, being late for class is not one of them. A check of my watch informed me that I would have to hoof it. Kicking October leaves and admiring the fall foliage would have to happen another time. Dodging college co-eds rushing to and from class would have to substitute for my mental respite this morning.

Usually, these walks helped me put my thoughts in order, or better yet, allowed me to detach myself from the events, both professional and private, that resided somewhere beyond my control. In class, I'd been called out more than once for having detached myself by way of crashing a game of catch on the quad, feeding the campus squirrels, and power napping on the Simpson College benches.

"I'm just taking in all that campus life has to offer," I would say.

"Yeah right, professor," I would usually hear in reply, the sarcasm thick and angsty. "Tell us another one."

"Well, in the immortal words of Socrates, 'An unexamined life is not worth living.'"

I just so happened that I would be referencing Socrates again in a matter of minutes. The plan for my 9:00 a.m. Introduction to Philosophy class was to follow up on a lesson I'd assigned the previous week, one that asked my students to produce a plausible usage for the words "why" or "why not" as they related to the status quo. In preparation, we had discussed the tale of Greek philosopher Socrates and his ill-fated attempt to set the record straight with an Athenian jury of his peers. Trying to beat the rap, Socrates claimed he had incited and corrupted the restless Athenian youths only under the guise of their right to worship as they pleased. Now, as I openly jogged to make it to class on time, I could only hope that, in the end, the whole thing would wind up better for me than it did for Socrates.

Even from the moment I flung open the door to the classroom, it was clear that my hopes would go for naught. My watch said I'd had them waiting for all of three minutes, but already, the ennui had settled in.

"He lives," someone said.

A smattering of chuckles followed as I hurried to the front of the class and began spreading out my notes.

"Apologies," I said, still catching my breath.

That no one replied set me slightly on my heels. There in a classroom short of natural light and long on painted beige, adorned with Formica tables and stackable plastic chairs, twenty-nine pairs of eyes blinked back at me. It would have been thirty, had Mark Birch not been openly dozing.

"Mr. Birch," I said, "will you be joining us this morning?"

"Until a minute ago," he replied, eyes still closed, "I was wondering the same thing about you, Professor."

Even I had to join in the laughter this time. "Not bad, Mr. Birch. Now if we could get on with it."

A great, reluctant shuffling followed, and a few seconds later, all thirty students had arranged themselves into something at least resembling a posture suggesting readiness to learn.

Flustered though I'd been, I immediately experienced a racing of excitement. I had created this assignment so my students could appreciate and respect the power of words and the value of finding truth and devotion to what truly mattered in life. More importantly, I wanted them to do as Socrates once did: value what it took to uphold their convictions whenever the status quo became adrift, complacent, and full of contradictions. I wanted these young people to embrace the notion that standing pat and in place, accepting the way things were, and not saying a word or doing something about it, was not something to accept in their daily lives.

To get them on proper footing, I had assigned them Plato's *Apology*. This text detailed three of Socrates's famed speeches at his trial for false wayward teaching and heresy.

"So, I assume you've all had a chance by now to get to the library and read the speech?" I said, addressing the class.

Roger Warren, slouching in his usual seat at the end of the front row of desks, chuckled.

"You found the speech amusing, Mr. Warren?"

He cleared his throat and straightened. "Not the speech exactly."

"Then what, exactly, did you find so funny?"

"Well, let's just say the librarian had some very interesting things to say about you, Professor Dolan." He shot a self-satisfied glance at Mark, his partner in crime, who sat to his right.

"Oh? And does Mr. Birch care to elaborate?" I smiled through gritted teeth as an image of the librarian, Carla Sanderson, came up in my mind.

"She said something like, 'I see Professor So-and-so is at it again with his why-or-why-not assignment.'"

I shook my head, smiling. Mark's impression of Simpson's senior research librarian could only be described as stunningly accurate, in both tone and inflection.

As laughter rippled through the room, I leaned back against my desk. It wasn't that I didn't have respect for the woman. She was well over sixty and still going strong, having lived through the Great Depression, World War II, and the Cold War. Still, I bristled as I recalled her words to my last-semester students: "Professor So-and-so should stick to physics!"

"Okay, okay." I came away from the desk. "Let's not get sidetracked."

The moment the words escaped my lips, I regretted them. Another thing I'd learned in more than twenty years of teaching was that the moment you hear yourself saying, "Let's not get sidetracked," it's already too late.

"You know there weren't enough copies of *The Apology* for all of us, right?"

I straightened up. For Denise Tate, a reserved and usually soft-spoken freshman, to speak up at all, let alone in a tone like this, meant that everyone in the room would be spitting nails. On top of it all, I actually *hadn't* known there wouldn't be enough copies.

"None of you have heard of a copy machine?" I quipped.

One after another, the students filled me in on how they'd found only fifteen copies of Socrates's immortal words stapled, stacked, and safely secured at the reference desk (labeled with big words in red: *Do not take*). Since the copier was broken and no one was around to fix it, they each had to take turns reading from the speech. Some students even resorted to taking the staples out and passing pages down the line to finish on time before the library closed.

"Well, I'm glad to hear you all demonstrated such resilience and willingness to adapt," I said, tongue firmly in cheek. "The question before us, though, is, what could the words 'why' or 'why not' mean?"

Tripping over my words with my students in class was nothing new. In fact, my own days as an undergraduate were not exactly free of controversy. The axiom "live by the sword, die by the sword" fit my time as a university student and later as a college professor nicely. Whether it was my words metaphorically throwing swords or my actions, I was never one to sit still and let things pass me by, especially events that had a moral or ethical connotation to them. My days as a young, energetic, and enthusiastic university student came to symbolize and represent many of my generation who took up their crosses as the radicals of the 1960s. Tens of thousands of other college and university students, myself included, were no longer going to sit by and let the establishment enjoy a free pass for not addressing issues related to civil rights, campus free speech, social and economic justice, and the Vietnam War.

"I have a question," Mark said abruptly. He was leaning aggressively to one side, his eyes drifting shut again. Not for the first time, I found myself marveling at how this young man always managed to do just enough to get by in a freshman-level prerequisite as a first-semester junior.

"Enlighten us, Mr. Birch," I said through a forced smile.

"The librarian said we should ask you where your challenge of the status quo got you as an undergraduate in 1964."

With a sigh, I looked down at my shoes. Some might have found it hard to believe, but as a college professor, I did not always celebrate being a 1960s campus radical. Ironically, in my profession, I was paid to focus on others' mistakes and glean valuable lessons from them, or at least try to.

"That sounds like a question from Mrs. Sanderson," I said evasively. "You said *you* had a question."

Mark gave a cockeyed smile. "Yeah, so, like, what did she mean?"

So, this was how a simple assignment and a snide research librarian wound up boxing me in. I am not one to shortchange my students. I decided to tell them my side of the story in the hope they would see their professor was, in some ways, just like them at their age at one point in his life.

I walked across the classroom and looked out the window at the quad. It was like looking into a mirror of sorts. I turned to the class and took them back to my days at Baker University in the fall of 1964. I recounted my days as campus radical standing up to the "status quo."

2

THE SIEGE

"The secret of happiness, you see, is not found in seeking more, but in developing the capacity to enjoy less."

—Socrates

Baker University, 1964

"Picture me as an undergraduate at Baker University on the West Coast in the early 1960s," I told my class, "A wide-eyed, slightly disheveled kid trying to find his way between his freshman and sophomore years."

From the looks I received, some of them seemed

to be having trouble imagining me at their age. I didn't let this deter me, because after all, even if she hadn't intended it, Mrs. Sanderson had provided me with the perfect opportunity to demonstrate what it meant to challenge the status quo.

"Kennedy's election to the presidency left an indelible mark," I continued, "and how could any of us ignore the images on TV of police dogs biting protesters and water hoses being turned loose on innocent bystanders? Young people, and specifically college students, were left wondering what kind of world we had inherited from our parents."

This notion seemed to land with them. Subtly, heads began to nod. Even Mark Birch sat at attention. No one took notes, I noticed, their hands resting idle on or under their desks.

"Quickly, I found myself captivated by the energy and enthusiasm of the student youth movement—not just any movement, but a movement that would start a wave of activism that lasted over a decade." As was often the case when I discussed this period of my life, I'd gotten ahead of myself. So, I stood to my full height and began pacing as my background delivered into focus. "I grew up Catholic and had strong moral leanings toward social and racial justice and affiliated causes. So, when I moved to California and enrolled as a transfer student, I of course joined a campus socialist club active in local causes. It wasn't long before I was helping protest unfair labor practices for Mexican farm laborers and African Americans in menial jobs. For my determined attempts, I was arrested and jailed, along with others, for trespassing on private property while protesting."

Now the eyes went wide. This wasn't the first time I'd held a 9:00 a.m. lecture in thrall, but it had been a while, and the thrill of it had my heart pounding.

"In jail, I met other student activists from nearby colleges and universities. We talked into the wee hours of the night and discussed the important work we were doing and the impact we were so passionate about making. These wee-hour talks would lead me to join a group of students going to Mississippi to assist local civil rights activists."

To my surprise, a dozen or so of the students picked up their pens and started taking notes without having to be told to do so. Nothing about this story would be necessary for their essays or tests, but I let them scribble away anyway.

"In the summer of 1964, we took a stance against the disenfranchisement of the Black vote in the Jim Crow South. We organized a get-out-the-vote drive to sign up as many African Americans as possible. We also involved ourselves in educational pursuits, like starting up summer schools to tutor young students in the three Rs (reading, writing, and arithmetic). In Black communities in Mississippi, the schools were woefully understaffed, poorly run, and lacking the basic resources to educate young children."

My students sat in rapt attention as I described the coming-out party that was the summer and fall of 1964. Along with thousands of other students returning to college that year, I had been inspired to take a stand against the status quo on campus. I joined the Student Nonviolent Coordinating Committee (SNCC) and Congress for Racial Equality (CORE), and later, stood at the forefront of the Free Speech Movement (FSM).

"Along with other students, I was no longer willing to sit idly by, basking in the comfort and security of academic life," I explained, and it wasn't lost on me, the potentially self-defeating nature of saying this to thirty students in an academic setting. "Sadly, my enthusiasm, together with other members, was tempered by the university regents, who were largely conservative and pushing for their universities to remain apolitical. They banned all campus political activity and fundraising, regardless of the cause or the promotion of civil participation for the greater good."

The shaky hand of Denise Tate slowly rose.

"Miss Tate," I said, unable to keep the surprise out of my tone.

"Doesn't that, um, violate the First Amendment?" she asked demurely.

"A very good point, Miss Tate," I said as I rounded my desk and took a seat. "And you're right, the First Amendment was not something the students and faculty would surrender to the Baker administration so easily. Just like Socrates, we weren't about to let officials hold us to a different intellectual standard in the name of law and order."

"So, like, did you start a riot or something?" This was from Roger Warren, who smirked as he spoke.

"Not exactly," I said, leaning back in my chair. "At least not at first."

The air in the room seemed to shift. No one made a sound.

"It was a fellow CORE member named Max who

first decided to directly challenge the university rule banning campus political activity and fundraising," I said.

I went on to explain how Max had set up a table in front of Hancock Hall, the campus library, to pass out civil rights literature and collect money for upcoming events. No sooner had he gotten the table upright than a campus police officer came by and told him to break it down. Max laughed the police officer off and kept on setting up his table.

The officer bristled and told Max that if he didn't vacate within five minutes, he would be arrested for unlawful assembly and trespassing. "I will call for backup if I must. If that happens," the officer promised, "things will get nasty."

"To Max's way of thinking," I revealed to my class, "given the cop's frame—overweight from too much coffee and donuts at the student union—how nasty could it reasonably get?"

Laughter rippled.

"So, the warning went in one ear and out the other," I continued, detailing how Max decided to sit down and put his feet up on the table to demonstrate his defiance and resolve on behalf of civil rights in

America. As devout Congress for Racial Equality (CORE) member, he was putting words into action. More specifically, Max was using direct action to help advocate for the end discriminatory practices in America. He was one of scores of students who were inspired by Gandhi's satyagraha concept of "firmness in a good cause."

Not to be outdone, the police officer strode over to the campus call box and phoned it in, shaking his head the whole time.

"Damn kids," he muttered to himself as he walked back toward the lawbreaker.

Soon enough, a campus police car rolled up with reinforcements. Max was handcuffed and placed in the back of the squad car. However, a couple of Baker students witnessed the whole scene, and soon, they came to Max's aid.

The students surrounded the squad car, barring it from leaving.

"Sit down!" someone yelled.

En masse, eight students trained in the art of nonviolent protesting sat down. Soon, they were joined by ten others.

With Max in the back seat, handcuffed and kept at

bay by the second police officer, the first officer addressed the mob. "Kids, I don't want to cause you any harm. This guy broke the campus soliciting rules. Please get on your feet and disperse at once."

Back in the present of my classroom, a tall, blond senior said, "Sir, we get the rules and all, but isn't it time someone challenged them for the greater good? Besides, there's a First Amendment right at play here."

Denise grew rigid with pride at having led us here. I gave her a soft smile and returned to describing the scene.

"Oh God," the officer retorted. "All I need is a would-be lawyer in the making to deal with."

"I don't need a law degree to know my rights."

"Son, I do *not* need a civics lesson. This student broke the rules, and I'm taking him in now, whether you like it or not. I have to take a leak, and my shift ends in sixty minutes. My wife's waiting on me, and I do *not* want to make her angry."

The senior looked the officer up and down, then glanced back at his compatriots. "Fine," he said. "If you have to piss and clock out, then you can go. But the squad car stays."

A stare-down ensued. Finally, the frustrated

officer exited to the library to take care of his business while Max and the other officer stood idly by.

The second officer was younger, thinner, and seemed much less annoyed by the sit-in. "Son, what are your plans here?" he asked, arching an eyebrow. "Are you going to let us do our job or what?"

The self-appointed lead of the protest looked over at his group and motioned for a chat. Noisily, they huddled, still blocking the car's path, and held a vote. With their heads pressed so close together in hushed tones and whispers, they somehow came to a quick resolution.

After the vote, the leader returned. "Sir, we've decided to detain this car until our demands are met." He steeled himself as he returned the police officer's piercing gaze.

"What?" the officer said.

"Our demands," the blond leader clarified.

The skinny officer quivered under a wave of disbelief and laughter. "What demands? This siege of yours just started five minutes ago. How in the world could you have produced anything already?"

The blond student shrugged. "Have it your way, sir. This car isn't going anywhere until our demands are met."

With Max in the back seat, the verbal siege continued, followed by each student giving a rousing, five-minute-long speech. The display helped rally their cause, encouraging other students to join. By 10:00 a.m., the protest numbered over a hundred students. By 10:30, it was two hundred. By noon, more than five hundred.

As the numbers swelled, additional campus police joined in, with the help of the president's office. Several administrators made their way to the squad car to check things out. To their amazement, both Max and the second police officer were in the back seat eating sandwiches and drinking pop.

"The protesters had decided to be civil during the siege," I pointed out. "They recognized that the true enemy wasn't the campus police, but rather, the university regents."

I looked out at my class and sought some sort of affirmation. It was returned to me with attentive silence. Finally, from the back of the classroom, a sharp student named Marie Olmstead piped up. "So where did you fit into all of this, professor?"

I took a deep breath and walked to the classroom

window once again. Out on the quad, leaves fell, foot traffic had picked up considerably, and all the stately buildings framed the autumn moment in a particular splendor. I swallowed and muttered, "Here we go, going backward again." I turned back to the class with a clever idea about where to start and a guarded fear about where it could end up.

Keeping an eye on the clock, I told them about how I showed up with reinforcements shortly after the Hancock Hall demonstration had begun. For several weeks, I had been working with other students on a list of demands to the university president, and by the time of the demonstration, it had taken the form of a manifesto. Max's detention and the student siege of the campus police car had sparked the perfect opportunity to present our arguments. These included a relaxation of the ban on political activity on campus, fundraising, and the passing out of various literature.

"Collectively, we felt as though we weren't asking for the moon," I explained to my class, "but rather, just for a place on campus to speak, hold rallies, and solicit donations in a noncombative fashion. To our way of thinking, this was an issue of free speech as it applied to the United States Constitution. Besides, is it not the mission of any university to foster free thinking, free speech, and the sharing of knowledge by all those who attend and teach there?" I took a pause, thinking about how these ideas were just as true twenty years later as when I was young. Then, I continued with my rendition of memories. "Shortly after I arrived, several students from the crowd chanted, 'Patrick, speak. Get up there and speak. Let them have it!'"

As I revealed these details to my Introduction to Philosophy students, I couldn't help but think of my younger self. A tall frame, a full head of hair, and a shabby beard, standing proud and direct in front of hundreds of Baker University students. To calm my nerves, I took a big, deep breath and surveyed the crowd and the setting. Close to eight hundred students had gathered in front of Hancock Hall.

"Believe it or not, speaking in front of large crowds was not my forte," I told my students. "Small settings, yes; big ones, no. All eyes were on me, or so it seemed."

Back to my retelling of the scene, as I moved toward the front, my fellow students parted and let me pass. Their silence was eerie. A few reached out and patted me on the back. I felt the weight of the moment as if the entire student body was perched upon my shoulders.

I looked around for a spot to speak from without luck. "On the top of the cop car!" one student yelled. I shrugged and glanced around to see how to mount the hood.

"Hold on right there, young man," said the overweight campus police officer, who'd apparently decided to enjoy some overtime rather than clock out and get home to his wife. "If you're going to do it, do it right. Do *not* damage my car." He motioned toward the trunk and said he had a stepladder in the back. "I use it to change the light bulbs in the campus call boxes," he said when he noticed my befuddled expression.

"And so," I told my students, who were looking more surprised and impressed with every new piece of the story, "I accepted the stepladder, took off my shoes, and climbed to the top of the police car. The view was quite impressive. Of course, it was. I was standing in front of several hundreds of my fellow students, a sea of faces focused on me."

Even as I stood as a professor before my philosophy class, I felt myself transported back to 1964. My pulse racing, I could practically feel the wind in my hair as I addressed the audience.

"Think back to when you were deciding to go to college," I said, my voice shaky with nerves as I called out loudly enough for all to hear. "Think about your expectations back then. No matter what happens today, we will keep civil. We can't give the administration anything to hang over our heads."

The applause that followed chased away what remained of my nervousness.

"As American citizens, you have a constitutionally protected *right* to express yourself nonviolently," I said. "Yours is the right to free thought and free speech." Over the cheering, I belted, "Today's protest represents a moral stance fostered by an obligation to do the right thing, at the right time, and for all the right reasons."

I pointed over to the second campus squad car that had arrived since the protests began. It was in this car that Max was now being held.

"Our brother's detention and proceedings against his stance to set up a table, pass out literature, and take collections represent an invocation of Baker University's conscience of a community," I argued. "This community started with its students and made its way upward to the administration. Freedom of thought and freedom of speech are the hallmark of a university education, and it was their right to demand the protection of that effort."

A wild cheer went up.

"If they—and indeed, if *we*—do not take a stance, the bureaucrats will continue to turn this university into a factory that mass-produces students for the marketplace and not the town square. We must return this community to the spirit of that town square, the place where the problems of society are challenged and fixed for the benefit of all."

Contrary to the feedback I'd been getting to this point, as I dismounted the squad car, you could hear a pin drop. I'd just started to think that I had somehow flubbed the end of the speech when, suddenly, rising up from somewhere in the back of the crowd, someone began chanting my name.

"Patrick! Patrick! Patrick!"

Soon, everyone was chanting in unison. Completely drained, I slipped out of the crowd. I just wanted to sit down, drink some water, and gather my thoughts. More importantly, I wanted to savor the moment, for I knew it had been special.

Even as I stood in front of my thunderstruck

philosophy class, I could still hear the cheers from my fellow Baker students who had assembled. So lost had I been in the moment that I had to take a few seconds to regroup and bring us all back to the present. The retelling of my own challenge to the status quo some thirty years removed had jarred me.

"Professor Dolan?" someone said. "Are you okay?"

In a hushed tone, "I muttered I guess so." I looked at the clock and dismissed my class.

3

CAMPUS STROLL

"Falling down is not failure. Failure comes when you stay where you have fallen."
—Socrates

"Way to go, Professor!" Ronny Jefferson exclaimed from the back of the room. An offensive tackle on the football team, Ronny wore a letterman's jacket and was built like most of his fellow linemen: big hands, broad shoulders, and no neck. "You were the man back in the day!"

I glanced at the clock behind me. We were nearly out of time.

Brenda Weiss, a bespectacled girl in the front row, raised her right hand.

"Yes?" I said with a nod.

"Were you afraid you might get arrested or kicked out of school?"

I drew back, momentarily flummoxed. "Good question." I thought for a moment, doing my best to recapture how I had felt that day, now long since passed. "I was definitely intimidated by talking to such a big crowd, but I don't remember worrying about what might happen. I was young—like all of you. I don't think I gave too much thought to the future." I chuckled. "Back then, I more or less thought I was invincible."

Everyone laughed. It was clear my story had grabbed their attention. But they were growing restless. I wasn't the only one stealing glances at the clock.

All I could do was smile. "Looks like we're out of time. I'll see you folks tomorrow."

With that, the students began gathering their things. Some, still captivated by the story, exchanged comments.

"Imagine not being able to organize on campus,"

Brenda said to Denise, rising beside her, as she slung her backpack over her shoulder.

"Yeah, that's lame," Denise replied. "I always thought anyone could protest. I mean, it's not my thing. But if someone wanted to stage a rally or something, I always thought all you had to do was get a permit or whatever."

The students, still buzzing, began to drift out. But Mark Birch looked like he wanted to keep the conversation going. I joined him as we exited the classroom into the crisp October air.

"Would you do it again?" he asked.

"Protest?"

"Yeah."

It seemed I had piqued my students' interest.

"Certainly," I said.

"What about now?"

"Now?"

Mark grew more animated, gesturing with his hands as we walked side by side. "Yeah, like, if something was happening now that you didn't agree with. Would you protest even though you're a professor?"

An intriguing question, I thought. "Perhaps. I

suppose it would depend on the issue and whether or not I felt it was being given a fair hearing."

"Cool," Mark said. He looked like he was about to ask another question but spotted some friends playing hacky sack in the quad and turned toward them. "See you around, Professor."

I gave him a wave and continued on my way. If my students asked again about my college exploits, it appeared unlikely that they would let me off the hook, even if I demurred. A small part of me felt protective about my past, in that I wasn't sure how much I wanted to divulge. But another part—a far *bigger* part—was eager to share my experiences. I knew from undergrad days the value of humanizing myself for my students. A relatable professor inspired students to dig deeper, engage more earnestly, and get the most out of their classes.

Like most days, I was in no hurry to get to my office. Grading tests and essays could wait. Instead, I preferred to walk to the student union building for a cup of coffee and maybe a slice of pizza. I enjoyed my campus strolls, which gave me an opportunity to court potential students, chat with fellow staff members, and, better still, get lost in my thoughts while using my feet. I typically did my best thinking when the rubber hit the road. But often my walks brought me into contact with my students outside of class, which could lead to some rather interesting conversations, obviously, ones that went beyond the materials taught in class.

Typically, you'll find four types of people on campus. The first type is extroverted students. Then there are the punctual ones on their way to class, those who are habitually late, and the select few who have prioritized fresh air and other concerns over their obligation to attend class. I try not to impede any of them for fear of interrupting their progress, academic or otherwise. A friendly hello or "How are you doing?" is standard fare. But I've been known to hold court during my walks and will greet a group of students who want to engage in some intellectual pursuits or seem open to a chat of some sort.

Sure enough, I spotted a familiar face just up ahead. Murphy, a freckle-faced student with a loping stride, looked surprised to see me. Dressed in a rugby shirt, Levi's, and mocha-brown Top-Siders, he was walking with a group of fellow undergraduates and paused to say hello. "Professor Dolan, how's life treating you?'"

"Not bad, Murphy," I said, nodding to his friends. "I sure missed you in my one p.m. class last Friday. Something more pressing must have come up. It wouldn't be that cute redhead I saw you draped all over in the student union, would it?"

Murphy, reddening, couldn't resist a retort. It was that or look bad in front of his friends. "Professor," he said with a shrug and a smile, "you know how you always tell us to seek knowledge and wisdom outside of the classroom and to enjoy life before it passes us by? Well, I took you up on it and decided to take matters into my own hands. Great advice! In fact, I took the liberty to discuss these recent endeavors with my crew here."

The chorus of laughter from Murphy's posse only led to more back-and-forth banter. All I could do was shake my head and laugh. Encounters like this one never failed to remind me why I loved teaching. I found enjoyment and solace in being an influence in and out of the classroom. And I never knew how it would start or end. My students sometimes gave me more than I gave them.

I continued toward the student union building

and spotted Alison Anderson, another undergrad, sitting alone on a bench and reading a book under a maple tree whose leaves were turning crimson. Alison belonged to what I consider the second type of person on campus: the loner. Dressed in muted colors and an oversized wool coat, she looked like she wanted to be invisible—or at least indistinguishable from her fellow students.

I stopped a few feet from the bench and waited for her to look up. When she did, she squinted her hazel eyes against the sun, which hung in the sky behind me.

"How's the book coming along?" I asked. It was always good to see students reading outside of class.

She gave me a bewildered look—a typical response—followed by a nod of approval. "I like it."

I noted the author (Toni Morrison) and the title (*Sula*). "Have you read anything else by Morrison?"

She shook her head no, and I could tell by her curt response that she was enjoying her quiet moment alone and was eager to return to her book.

"Well," I said, convinced it was time to move on, "enjoy!"

I resumed my stroll, satisfied that another young mind had found inspiration. I cared about every individual and the student body at large. Why else would I have gotten into the profession? It certainly wasn't for the money or so-called public adoration.

I had almost reached the student union building when I crossed paths with Helen Beauchamp, a university administrator and member of the third type of person populating the campus. Dressed in a long skirt and sweater, her graying locks cropped short, Helen looked the part. She was an administrator right down to the sensible orthopedic shoes supporting her arches and the reading glasses dangling from her neck.

Helen and I served on the same curriculum committee, which meant I was obligated to acknowledge her now that we'd made eye contact.

"Ah," I said, searching for something to say. "Good to see you, Helen."

"And you as well, Professor Dolan."

Had she not looked up, I would have blazed past— always my goal when encountering an administrator or fellow faculty member on campus. But here I was, caught in a conversation. The next words spoken would have to come from her. I never initiated more than a cordial greeting. At least she wasn't the college president or provost, I told myself. Then again, spying either on campus would have been the equivalent of a UFO sighting. It didn't take a rocket scientist—or even a philosopher—to figure out why the administration parking lot sat adjacent to the back door exits of buildings removed from higher learning. Students typically saw administrators on two days: the first day during student orientation and the last day at graduation. Any time in between was relegated to fundraising.

Helen was more likely to get lost on campus—not an unusual event for an administrator—than interact with students. "I don't think I've seen you since the last committee meeting," she said, letting the words linger like an invitation to dance.

"Yes." I cleared my throat. She was going to make me work. "You made an excellent summation at the last meeting. I like how things are progressing." I feigned a look at my watch. "Well, I better get moving. Always nice catching up with you."

The less I saw of the higher-ups and the less I said, the better.

"You too!" she called after me as I raced toward the entrance to the student union building.

I stepped inside to see a group of about a dozen

people gathered near the information desk, where a student volunteer dispensed bus tokens, campus maps, candy, and any number of odds and ends. The group—half prospective students and half parents—represented the final type of campus goer. They were essentially tourists, here to get a good look at the place. But they were led by an actual student, in this case an able young woman I had taught the previous year.

"Hi, Professor Dolan!" she said with a wave.

I paused long enough to ready my lines. "Hello." I eyed the eager parents and their somewhat less enthusiastic offspring. "Great to have all of you on campus today. I hope you enjoy your tour."

Had I been pressed for more, I might say something to the prospective students like, "You can't go wrong coming to our college," or, "I look forward to having you in one of my classes." But today no one asked a question or appeared needful of further attention, so I kept moving, determined not to impede their progress. The last thing I wanted to do was say something that might be taken out of context. In any case, I had an excuse at the ready—"I'm late to class (or a meeting) and need to get going"—should anyone insist on starting a conversation. After all, I wasn't an expert on the topics they were hoping to explore during their tour: tuition costs, campus safety, job opportunities after graduation, and so forth.

I continued on to the coffee shop, which I considered the heart and soul of our campus. Like the quad, it served as a gathering place, buzzing with pleasant energy, and proved that life did, in fact, continue outside the classroom. In contrast, the library, less than a two-minute walk from the counter where I waited for my straight black coffee, was a place of solitude and regeneration for many students. Not just a place to locate books and research important documents or holdings to write a term paper, the library gave students somewhere to escape the academic rat race. I often disappeared into the stacks to find a cozy chair and catch a few winks before a late-afternoon class.

But back to the student union building, which, like the quad, had less to do with academics and more to do with socializing. Outside on the quad, students strolled together or played touch football or Frisbee. Here, they sequestered in the coffee shop's cozy confines to sip coffee, break bread, and converse. If the quad served as the center of the university's universe, a strategic place around which all other happenings revolved, academic or otherwise, the student union building and its coffee shop and food court invited students and faculty members alike into a deeper, more nourishing experience of campus life. Little did I know just how true the Simpson student union's purpose in campus life and meaning would play out in the days to come.

4

CAMPUS BENCH THERAPY

**"The secret of happiness, you see, is not found
in seeking more, but in developing the
capacity to enjoy less."
—Socrates**

"So, Professor, did Socrates hold up?"

I tore my gaze from a family of squirrels making
their way up and down a hundred-year-old oak at the
edge of the quad to find a gangly young man with a
head full of unruly dark hair, grinning down at me.

"I . . . I guess so," I said, taking a sip of my coffee.

He shrugged off his backpack and held it at his

side. "Mind if I sit?"

So much for my own private oasis. I scooted to one side of "my" bench, where I liked to sit and contemplate each afternoon after class. I called it "bench therapy," which I used to think through the events of the day or, better yet, think about general things. I had learned a long time ago from an older professor not to get so caught up in the job that you forget to process things in and out of the classroom. I had found that doing so kept me fresh, not only for the sake of sanity but also for my students. I tried hard to make things informative, engaging, and relevant in my lectures and related coursework.

"I don't mean to be rude," the kid said. "My roommate is in your philosophy class. He told me about the Socrates assignment."

"I see. And your name is?"

"Oh, sorry." He extended a hand, his long fingers matching his rangy frame. "Jeremy Stiles— sophomore."

"Patrick Dolan."

"Oh, I know your name, Professor." Jeremy unzipped his pack, pulled out a shiny green Granny Smith apple, and polished it on his cargo shorts. "I actually signed up for your class and then had to drop it due to a scheduling conflict. The way my roommate has been going on about the Socrates assignment, though, I wish I'd dropped sociology instead."

Not one to turn down accolades, I smiled. "Thank you."

In fact, I'd just been thinking about the assignment. As much as I was frustrated by the mix-up on the number of copies made and the difficulties my students had faced in completing the reading, the reference librarian's comment about me challenging the "status quo" had upset me the most. I typically didn't bring my past into the classroom. Yes, I did have some positive aspects of my past to share, but most of my undergraduate, graduate, and associate faculty days had proved problematic. Most of it was tied to my undergraduate days as a campus radical. Some who knew of my past wanted to hear all about it. Others wanted nothing to do with me. I was mostly treated as an outcast, neither given trust nor equal footing. The stink of being a campus radical had followed me for years. As the saying went, once a troublemaker, always a troublemaker.

"Professor," Jeremy said, his eyes narrowing at

the distance, "do you have any regrets about your days as a campus radical?"

I gave a soft smile. "None that I can think of, at least when looking at my twenty-year-old self. But as a grown adult who has lived and experienced the ebbs and flows of life, I have what I call reservations."

He cocked his head to one side, curious.

"I was inspired to make a difference and promote change," I explained. "But I had no clue about starting a movement or the consequences that resulted. As a professor, I teach the value of being cynical and to question things, but it stops there. I do not advocate the destruction of property, interrupting university and college operations, and threatening staff members in the name of righting a so-called injustice or a good cause."

He nodded his understanding.

"More to the point, what starts out typically looking good on paper in an ad hoc fashion can take on a life of its own if the wrong type of people get involved. Our protest at Baker was peaceful and respectful, but as it spread to other campuses, it became more radical, more forceful, and most certainly violent. I didn't sign up for that, nor did a lot of my peers. That's why I dropped out. The wrong type of people took up the cross and outside agency took over."

"So, what's the alternative then?" he asked. "How do you keep a peaceful protest from becoming violent and destructive to the sanctity and mission of the university?"

"Try this on for size: First off, professors and administrators must keep the academy open to free speech and debate that goes against or challenges to the status quo. In other words, dissent and protest is okay, provided that it's peaceful, respectful, and dignified. By all means, it must set the example for others to follow—especially if it leaves the confines of the hallowed halls for society at large."

The thoughtful student looked at me and asked, "So what's the right way for any student to look at a protest before joining?"

"The first thing a student should be doing is asking a lot of questions. For example, who are the leaders of this protest? What skin do they have in the game? How committed are they to seeing the protest through to the end? Other questions include: What exactly are they protesting? Is the resolution of the protest worth the consequences if it fails? What resources are being employed to see the protest succeed?"

"That's a lot of questions to be asked," he muttered. "Makes joining the movement or protest without thinking about it a lot easier."

I leaned forward and rested my elbows on my knees. "Let me leave you with this thought: Hindsight is twenty-twenty in life. If I would have asked these questions in 1964 at Baker, I'm not sure I would have joined or led the protest. My motivations came with me to Baker. I had already stood up for civil rights for African Americans in Mississippi and joined protests for migrants in California. I came to Baker already radicalized, and I moved to do the same on campus in a civil and orderly fashion. The tables have turned for me. My job as a professor is to not only help students identify the status quo and scrutinize its successes or failings, but to ask the immortal question, 'Is it worth saving or bringing it to end?'"

"That makes sense," he said.

"So, Jeremy," I said in a lighter tone, "what do you know about Socrates and his influence on Western civilization?"

He shrugged. "Not much. I've skimmed through some of your course materials when my roommate leaves them out, but he's really particular about people touching his stuff, so I have to be careful. But from what I can tell, he's a bit overrated."

I stifled a laugh. "Socrates? Overrated?"

"Yeah."

I couldn't resist the urge to counter such nonsense. "Socrates brought philosophy down to earth. He moved it from the abstract and obtuse to a more sensible plane—a body of knowledge concerned with man and his role in society. More importantly, he centered his teachings on morality and how it relates to absolutes instead of relative values affected by historical and social conditions. Sadly, it was this absolutism that got him into trouble with the Athenian elders."

"They put him on trial," Jeremy said.

"Right. He was brought up on three charges. The first was disrespecting the Greek gods. The second was subverting and corrupting young Athenians. The third and final charge was challenging the status quo with his line of inquiry after the war with Sparta. He literally walked the streets in Athens and asked his fellow citizens why they'd lost the war—a dangerous activity as far as the authorities were concerned."

Jeremy frowned. "But what makes him the final arbiter on everything? He's always talking about how everyone else speaks falsely, but we're supposed to believe him that *he's* the only one with real virtue, like he owns Truth with a capital *T*."

"No, that's not it at all," I countered. "Socrates admitted he knew nothing—something nobody around him, including the powers that be, dared to do. He started there, from his professed ignorance, and worked toward a greater understanding of the world."

I withdrew a chestnut from my pocket and tossed it to one of the squirrels flitting about beside the oak's stout trunk. The squirrels on campus were known to gather in class windows, seeking student handouts. I appreciated their company and was beginning to regret engaging Jeremy on a subject he clearly knew little about.

Jeremy remained unimpressed. "I'd rather read Nietzsche."

I laughed. "Of course you would. Nietzsche expressed strong criticisms of Socrates, by the way."

"Oh yeah? What did he say?"

"He said Socrates's philosophy was antilife."

"I get that," Jeremy said with a knowing nod.

I doubt it, I thought. I tried to bring us back to more factual terrain. "The only reason we know about Socrates and his teachings is because others wrote about him. His studies under Archelaus and Protagoras were passed on by his students, one of whom was Plato, a philosopher in his own right. Thanks to Plato, we know how Socrates thought about the function of morality, religion, and social and political issues as they relate to Greek life, which brings us full circle to the influence of Socrates. His ideas form the basis of Western philosophy. The Socratic dialogues, as they're called, have been read, studied, and debated for centuries."

I paused for a second, wondering if anything I was saying was sinking in for my new understudy. "What it boils down to is this: Socrates strove to find the essence of what it means to be a good citizen. His philosophy and teachings led to the creation of what we now call metaphysics and transcendental philosophy and its pursuits. These pursuits include inductive logic or inductive symbolism aimed at discovering universal and unchangeable truths. These truths provide the definition of justice and the pretext of law and order—the opposite of situational ethics based on the individual and his circumstances."

Jeremy slumped beside me, if not convinced, at least less strident in his views. "Well, that explains why you decided to give Socrates a go in your class." He shook his head as if to clear it and then stood. "I need to get going. I have class in fifteen minutes. But I'd like to crash your class sometime if you don't mind. You gave me a lot to think about. You certainly know your stuff. Of course, I want to hear about your campus revolt in 1964 as well."

My eyes widened. "Your roommate told you about that too?"

"Yup. Sounds like it was pretty wild."

I nodded as he left and then tossed another chestnut to the squirrels. It seemed my past was more intriguing to my students than the subject matter I was teaching. I would have to figure out how to use that to my advantage.

After a few more minutes, I took leave of this back-and-forth and headed back to my office and then home. I thought to myself, I would love to run into this young man again and engage in another enlightening conversation again, Socrates or not.

5

THE PHONE CALL

"Wonder is the beginning of wisdom."
—Socrates

Later that evening, I had just returned home from walking my dog, Socrates, who loved sauntering along the tree-lined streets of my quiet neighborhood, only a stone's throw from campus, when I spotted my elderly neighbor giving me the stink eye.

Gladys, dressed in a faded-pink bathrobe and armed with the stub of a cigarette, stood on her front porch next door and paused long enough to glare at me.

"Good evening, Gladys," I said, not bothering to

hide the derision in my voice. "It's always lovely to see you."

She rolled her eyes before stepping inside and slamming her front door shut.

Gladys had lost her overweight gray tabby a while back, and said cat had been found dead on my driveway. The paperboy had been the first to spot its bloated corpse and had alerted Gladys within moments of his gruesome discovery. Seconds later, she had stormed my front porch, interrogating me like she was the Grand Inquisitor.

I'd told her and everyone who would listen that I was innocent of the cat's murder, but not until someone stepped forward to admit they'd put out rat poisoning did my nosey neighbors stop calling me a cat killer. Cat Gate, as I liked to call it, belonged squarely in the past, but Gladys still held it against me. As far as she was concerned, I was still guilty, still a cat killer, regardless of the facts.

I followed Socrates onto my wraparound porch and stepped inside just in time to hear the phone ring. Life was pretty uncomplicated at home. I lived alone, hired a gardener to keep my big backyard tidy, and mostly spent quiet evenings grading papers, working on the latest syllabus, or whatnot. So when the phone rang, my ears perked up.

I had been married once, but like everything in my life, it had come and gone. Not everyone was cut out to be married to an academic, especially one like me who had been through hell and back trying to climb the ivory tower. I didn't doubt that I'd made the right career choice, but it had cost me personally. My nose has always been buried in books and my thoughts in the clouds as I sought the truths that had eluded others.

Looking back on it all, I realized my father had been right about the relationship between money and noble pursuits: One paid the bills, and the other led to poverty and heartache. My splitting the difference between physics and philosophy hadn't paid off financially, but I could go to sleep at night with a happy heart and a clear head. Getting paid to dispense "hot air" and lofty ideas for a living was like getting paid to breathe. It was something I was going to do anyway.

I hurried to the living room, where the phone sat on an end table next to the couch, and picked up on the fourth ring. "Hello?"

"Hey, it's Max."

I recognized Max Rothmann's distinctive baritone

immediately. His voice sounded subdued, like he was calling with bad news.

"What's going on? Is everything all right?"

"I'm afraid not. I have some bad news for you. Sarah Goldstein died."

I closed my eyes and gasped. I said nothing. I stood, stunned and thunderstruck, in silence.

"You there Patrick?" he said.

"Yeah, I'm here," I responded.

Sarah Goldstein, like Max, was a former classmate of mine at Baker University. Unbeknownst to me, she had been battling cancer for some time. Those close to her had been holding out hope she might somehow kick it. Max filled me in the best he could. He came right out and told me that he had known for a while but elected not to say anything. Once again, twice in one day my past was revisiting me, or better yet, pulling me backward.

Even as Max continued to talk, I was lost in my thoughts about Sarah. She had been more than a friend. She had been a lover and soulmate, someone who had changed my world forever. We had connected mentally, intellectually, and spiritually. Sadly, we had never buried the bones of our relationship. Nor had we healed the wounds. Closure had eluded me, and our breakup had haunted me ever since, affecting every relationship that followed, my marriage included.

"Will there be a service?" I asked.

"Yeah. They're planning a brief burial ceremony on Friday. "Are you ready for this?" Max said. "She wrote you a letter. I have it right here. You want me to mail it to you? Or would you rather come to Chicago and pick it up?"

I slumped down on the plush couch beside the end table. The mantle clock ticked steadily above the sooty fireplace in the otherwise silent living room. "Let me think about it."

My head was spinning. I'd have precious little time to arrange a flight to Chicago. I'd also have to make sure my classes were covered while I was gone. Max's request felt like a summons.

"Let me digest all of this and mull it over," I finally said. "Let me call you back in a few hours."

"Sure. I'll be here awaiting your call." Max replied.

After hanging up, I paced to the kitchen and stared into a mostly empty refrigerator without seeing anything. Nearly three decades had passed since Sarah and I had parted on less-than-amicable terms. We hadn't talked since. We met at school, participated in protests, joined activist clubs and organizations, and felt like we were made for each other. We both enjoyed books, long talks, putting up a good fight in the name of a better world, and denouncing the man. We were in lockstep with tens of thousands of other young college students of the 1960s. Our symbiotic relationship lasted fifteen months before falling flat on its face. I still wasn't sure what had happened in the end. All I knew was that she had left school for the summer, and I had never heard from her again. I wrote letter after letter seeking answers, but to no avail. I couldn't call because her number was unlisted.

Over the years, I had wondered what happened, but my therapist had told me, while sorting out other issues, to let it go. Her father, more abruptly, wrote me a letter insisting that I leave their daughter alone. Out of respect for Sarah, I decided to do as her father asked, walk away, and get on with my life.

I finally settled on some leftover pasta, still in the sauce pan I had prepared it in and transferred it from the refrigerator to the stovetop. As I warmed it up, I continued thinking about Sarah. Where had we gone wrong? What had pulled us apart? At the heart of it, I recognized, was my desire to step back from all the protesting. She wanted to continue, but I wanted no part of the violence that had begun to escalate in colleges and universities across America. The once-civil discourse and protests became chaotic and destructive as student and activist leadership fell apart. No one wanted to take ownership or seek common ground among the leadership councils. Sarah wanted a nationwide revolution. All I wanted was local action through nonviolent protest and civil discourse. Riots, destruction of property, and confronting police officers were not my cup of tea. I walked away, not wanting to end up with blood on my hands.

In retrospect, far too much had been made of my stance at Baker University in 1964. It seemed like everyone wanted a piece of me. Getting up on a police car, giving speeches, creating petitions, writing a manifesto—that was one thing. Traveling the country and sanctioning a more destructive path was another. I could not and would not deliver those things. Sarah wanted me to show courage and jump into the fray. From the fall of 1964 to the spring of 1965, she was the love of my life. But something happened before school let out.

When she didn't return to school, I tried calling her and writing letters to her to find out what was going on. I even thought of driving to Chicago but ultimately decided against it. I knew from previous conversations with her that her choice of a love interest hadn't exactly been a hit with her parents. She was Jewish, and her parents didn't want her to have anything to do with a Catholic boy in pursuit of social justice and lofty universal truths. I couldn't blame them. It wasn't a religious thing, per se; it was more that her parents wanted something that was, in their view, better for their daughter. By the following winter, I had let go and put Sarah in my rearview mirror. No one ever mentions that a rearview mirror has three sides: one mental, one spiritual, and one physical.

I called Max back around nine o'clock, still early for a night owl like me, and gave him my answer. "I'm coming."

"Great. How 'bout I pick you up at the airport? You're welcome to stay at my place." His voice, close to monotone earlier, had brightened considerably. "I'm glad you're coming, Patrick. I wish it was under better circumstances, but I'm looking forward to the reunion. So much has happened. We've got a lot of catching up to do."

It was true. Our career paths had taken us in opposite directions. He had chosen law, and I had opted for academia. But we had both forsaken our protest days, when he had been determined to stick it to the man and I had boldly denounced the academic machine. Now he was defending the man, and I was part of the system. I had chosen to work within the hallowed halls of academia, using my classroom to explore thoughts about the status quo. He had decided to defend it in a courtroom. While our paths had diverged, Sarah was the thread that connected us. Going to Chicago, in many ways, represented closure. At her funeral, I would say goodbye to someone who was still alive in my heart. And I would read the letter she had written me.

After I put the phone down, all I could do was to mutter once again, "What's with all this backward stuff?"

6

SHOEBOX FLASHBACKS

"To find yourself, think for yourself."
—Socrates

The news of Sarah's passing had me reaching for the past with mixed emotions. In the study closet, I found one of my shoeboxes full of old photographs, protest flyers, and letters from my Baker University days.

I had started storing memorabilia and other relics in shoeboxes at an early age, and the boxes usually ended up under my bed or on the top shelf in my closet. I stashed away baseball cards, important letters and photographs, family keepsakes, and other mementos, even long after they had lost their specialness. It would have taken an act of Congress to get me to throw them away. I found meaning in hanging on to physical things. Some, no doubt, would have called me sentimental. And, yes, my penchant for clinging to the past had gotten me into trouble over the past forty-five years.

Bundled in a neat stack and tied together by a fraying rubber band were several old letters. I had sent them to Sarah in the summer and fall of 1965, and each one had been returned to me unopened. Contained in the letters were words seeking a resolution or, failing that, an explanation for her disappearance and subsequent silence. After she had left Baker for the summer without a word, I had poured my heart out to her in hopes she would contact me and let me know what was happening. After a few months, I had given up pursuing her, concluding that it was best to let things go for a while in hopes she would return to school and me. Sadly, she never did, nor did I ever receive an explanation why.

I took the shoebox to my desk, and with trembling hands, slipped one of the letters from the bundle and opened it. The seal gave way easily, having dried out over the decades, and I tugged free the one-page letter inside. A wave of nostalgia washed over me as I stared at the words I had hammered out on my taupe-colored IBM Selectric so long ago. I could just make out where I had used Liquid Paper whiteout to erase a handful of typos.

Dear Sarah,

I'm hoping against hope that you open this letter. Every day that goes by without a response from you feels like another lost opportunity to find out what went wrong. Was it something I said or did? Something I failed to say or do?

Until I met you, I was perfectly content to lose myself in my studies. Books were my closest companions, words my sole obsession. I remember going to parties, seeing a cute girl, and thinking, "I've got more important things to do." It's not that I didn't enjoy a good time or that I wasn't a red-blooded male with typical wants and needs. I just felt preoccupied, I guess. I was restless.

Then I met you, and everything changed. You got me. Hell, you made me feel like you knew me better than I knew myself at times. Every time I stared into your eyes, I felt your soul staring back at mine. You knew what I wanted without me having to say it. You finished my thoughts. Even when we disagreed or argued, I got a charge out of our discussions. You made me grow and learn. You took me out of my comfort zone. You made me a better person.

So here I am, wondering what went wrong. I can't know if you won't talk to me. I can't know if all I hear from you is silence. If there's something I can do, something that needs mending or addressing, I can't know without a response from you. Talk to me. Please.

Yours forever,
Patrick

I folded the letter and returned it to its envelope, surprised at the letter's eloquence. I hadn't been much more than a kid at the time, yet here was proof that I had known my heart and had been able to express my feelings in an earnest, if unsuccessful, attempt at reestablishing communication. I shook my head to clear it. I was just getting started.

I was tempted to open another returned letter, but a faded Polaroid in the shoebox caught my attention.

The colors were washed out, everything cast in sepia tones. In the photo, I stood with my roommates and a couple of friends in the living room of our cramped apartment. Stacks of textbooks and paperbacks littered the floor. Beer cans were everywhere, most of them empty. A filmy yellow haze of cigarette smoke gathered near the ceiling. Even then, I thought, we were different. While others had been content to work joe jobs or run the family business, we'd striven for something more—even with the pall of the Vietnam War hanging over us. Each of us, in our own way, had wanted to rise above our circumstances and chart a unique course. The Polaroid was from another life, one that almost felt like it belonged to someone else. Yet in a strange way, I still felt connected to those days, as if hardly any time had passed. I was still the same person staring back at me, hopeless innocence masked by the bravado and swagger of my ambitions. As for the others in the photo, I recognized most of the faces immediately. Others, lost to time, eluded me.

What was the guy's name? How did I know him?

Each of us wore the uniform of those days: short hair, white Oxford shirts, comfortable cotton twill trousers that hugged our legs, and leather monk strap shoes. Some wore ties, others sweater vests. We weren't mods. We weren't that self-conscious. But we were cool—or so we thought. I could almost hear the Animals' "House of the Rising Sun" playing on the turntable, the sound of Alan Price's Vox Continental ringing out like a church organ.

Then I spotted another color photo of Sarah and me. We were standing on a sidewalk, learning against someone's sky-blue Chevy Bel Air, bare trees and leaden clouds just visible behind us. She wore a knee-length skirt and matching jacket, the latter with oversized buttons. She had long curly hair and a lovely figure, but it was her smile—always her smile—that fixed me. It radiated joy and warmth but also a sense of vulnerability that I found irresistible—even when she was smiling back at me from an ancient photo.

My mind raced from one memory to the next, and I found myself reminiscing about our late-night discussions on the Free Speech Movement, the ills of capitalism, marches on behalf of social and economic justice, the war in Southeast Asia, the arms race, and so much more. As I continued rummaging through the photographs, I was shocked to see so many faces of people that wouldn't survive the decade. Friends were drafted to fight in Vietnam and killed, fell into the trappings of drugs and alcohol, or dropped out altogether, never to be seen or heard from again.

After an hour's worth of recollections, I leaned back in my office chair and closed my eyes. My stroll down memory lane had knocked me for a sentimental loop. I found myself traveling back again to the fall of 1964 and the spring of 1965, for better or worse. Talking with my students about my days at Baker and my involvement in the Free Speech Movement was something I could do without too much difficulty. But when I had to make connections to my classmates and the people I'd grown quite fond of, especially Sarah, and when I thought about the unrealistic expectations that had been placed on me during that period in my life, I found my mood darken. I had actually dropped out of school for a couple of semesters in an attempt to get my head on straight and move on.

I closed the last of the shoeboxes, returned them to the closet, and carefully closed the closet door. As a philosophy professor who studied the past and implored his students to engage in self-reflection and introspection every day, I told myself I shouldn't have felt so much weight while revisiting the past. Who was

I to ask others to look backward in order to move forward if I wasn't willing to do the same?

It's more than abstract history, I thought as I switched off the overhead light. *It's personal.* Part of me didn't want to revisit Sarah's disappearance. Too much pain. Too much mystery. Too many unresolved matters of the heart. But her passing had forced a reckoning of sorts. I had no choice but to go backward in time and dig up what had been buried for so long. The alternative—blissful ignorance—had never been an option for me.

No matter what had transpired long ago, it was time to put it to rest. As the saying goes, you can run from the truth, but you can't hide from it. Going to Chicago to retrieve a letter from a long-lost love was my truth, or better yet, Sarah's truth, providing closure, for better or worse.

7

HAP

"Education is the kindling of a flame, not the filling of a vessel."
—Socrates

Socrates stared at me forlornly from the landing as I carried my overnight bag down the stairs. The dog knew when I was leaving. He just knew. I had arranged for a former student who lived nearby to house-sit and take care of him while I was gone, but Socrates, an Old English Sheepdog with a long salt-and-pepper mustache, was having none of it. Part sage, part grifter, Socrates knew how to work a room, whether it was for scraps, a belly rub, or in my case, a place to stay. He had a dopey grin and sad eyes that could melt the ice caps. Like most, I couldn't resist his charms.

"It's only for a few days," I told him as I made sure his collar was on snugly. "Kellie will be here soon. She's in charge while I'm gone. Behave. And don't go running off."

Socrates knew how to work Kellie. She had house-sat for me on a few occasions in the past. The dog was always a little plumper—and a little less inclined to follow direction—when I came home.

I gave Socrates one last pat on the head and then stepped outside with my overnight bag, making sure to lock the front door behind me. Gladys was sitting on her front porch swing, the embers of her cigarette glowing fiercely as she huffed smoke. I forced a smile but said nothing. Sometimes I just didn't have the energy to indulge her judgmental frown. And fortunately for me, Hap was waiting in his beat-up Oldsmobile out front.

Thelonious "Hap" Williams, known to Simpson College as a jack-of-all-trades, worked at the school as a research librarian, an ad hoc adviser to the president of the college, a part-time fundraiser, and an admissions clerk. There was nothing he wouldn't do to make Simpson a better place. The college administrators, staff, professors, and students all held him in high regard, and rightfully so.

"Morning, Professor," he said with a wry smile as I ducked inside his land boat, which smelled like the Royal Pine air freshener hanging like a Christmas ornament from the rearview mirror. He had agreed to take time out of his busy schedule to drive me to the airport. Hap was always good for a favor.

"Good morning yourself."

"Ready for your trip?"

"As ready as I'll ever be."

I was feeling distracted—the way I always felt when leaving town. But the knot in my gut could be traced to my apprehension about Sarah's funeral and the letter awaiting me. I was filled with equal parts excitement and dread. Closure was long overdue. Would I get it? Or would she put me off one last time, leaving me to ruminate until my dying days?

Hap was silent as we left the neighborhood, seemingly content to fidget with the knob that controlled his window wipers as a gentle rain began to fall. That was typical for him. He had a knack for knowing when to talk—and when not to pry into someone's personal business. He had his skeletons, and I had mine. In my case, it was an academic career that had been stunted by actions and words long ago, and in his case, it was being in the wrong place at the wrong time. To some extent, I deserved what I'd gotten. In Hap's case, he didn't.

- - -

I had met Hap years earlier after inadvertently leaving lecture notes on a chalkboard in Hickok Hall. On his way home, he noticed the classroom door ajar with the light left on and took the time to secure both. He read my notes before turning off the lights and locked the classroom door. The next day, he left a note in my mailbox suggesting I follow up my lecture by consulting several books and journal articles. Under normal circumstances, I would have offered a few choice words to the note giver, reminding him or her to stay out of my lectures and stick to doing whatever it was that they did—in this case, stocking the library shelves. But I was new to Simpson College at the time, so I elected not to make a big deal of it and avoided making waves.

Ego aside, I read the list and was intrigued by

several unfamiliar titles and journals. Impressed, I was interested in meeting this upstart. Yes, upstart. It was one thing to receive suggestions related to academic material from peers within my department but quite another to get them from a stranger. It wasn't that I considered librarians outliers; their skills and knowledge were typically cultivated over time and complemented what went on in the classroom. What made Hap's reading list different was that it helped shape the Socrates-related project I would go on to assign students for the next several years: asking the immortal question of why and its relationship to the status quo. Hap's suggestions helped bring Socrates, his dialogues, and his mode of inquiry to life for me and my students. Nevertheless, I was still struggling to apply it to modern times and the minds of my philosophy students.

I finally met Hap in person while returning books to the reference desk a few weeks after the semester ended. He stood tall behind the counter, a handsome, well-dressed Black man with a shit-eating grin.

"So, Professor," he began in a mellifluous voice, "have you found the essence of Socrates's immortal question of why and how it corrupted the Athenian youth and led to his death?"

I glanced at his name tag. "Mr. Williams, you could say I'm well on my way, thanks to your timely advice last semester. In fact, I've been meaning to track you down and thank you for the wonderful and inspiring note. Seeing that you work in a library surrounded by hundreds of thousands of books aimed at preserving knowledge and aiding the learning process, I'm sure you have even more suggestions for me, solicited or not."

He offered a hearty laugh—from the gut and wholly authentic.

"In fact," I continued, "I had quite a winter break, thanks to you. I took several of your suggestions with me on a visit to my parents' house in New Jersey. I always go to New York to a used bookstore called the Strand on Broadway Avenue in the East Village. I'm sure you've heard of it."

"I'm quite familiar with it," Hap said with a nod. "Did you happen to run into Gertrude Bell while you were there? She runs the place. I collaborate with her a fair amount on rare books when they become available. She's quite an asset to universities and colleges when it comes to rare and hard-to-find books. I've found in my dealings with her that it's not all business all the time. She has a soft spot for the learning process, since both her parents were educators."

I was impressed and felt I had to respond in kind. "If Ms. Bell is the same lady I see working the aisles and barking orders to her salespeople like a drill sergeant, she's most certainly still there." I had learned to avoid her like the plague. The fear in her employees' eyes told me everything I needed to know about her. "I keep my visits to the Strand brief. I don't want to come back with more books than I can manage. More than a suitcase full is too much for me. I could have them shipped back, but I like having my parcels with me."

Hap smiled knowingly. "There's a guy out West working out of his garage that plans to change all the face-to-face stuff when it comes to bookstores. He plans to ship books directly out of a warehouse to the customer. He's been cataloging titles and selling them that way for a while now. It'll be interesting to see how that all works out."

"Sounds interesting to say the least," I replied, trying to sound knowledgeable on the subject. I doubted the idea would ever get off the ground. Who would trade the bookstore experience for a soulless transaction in the mail? But I tried to maintain an open mind. "Selling out of a garage sounds novel to me. I hope he has lots of cardboard to protect those books traveling through the mail. I'm not a huge fan of receiving damaged goods in the mail, regardless of the item or cost. Besides, I love walking into bookstores and taking in the sights and smells. Looking for lost treasures on the shelves amounts to an adventure of sorts—one that I relish from start to finish. Passing my hand over the spine and cover and flipping to the back of the book to look at the author's bio feels like treasure hunting without a map. I love the journey, not the destination, when visiting bookstores."

I thanked Hap and turned to leave.

"I certainly see the value of bookstores and book hunting, Professor," he said. "I never left Simpson after I graduated. My love of books and learning as an undergraduate kept me young and enthralled all these years. Nothing like being paid to have an intellectual feast each and every day that includes books, knowledge, and a journey of the mind and soul."

He offered a hand, and I shook it, finding it firm and confident. I sensed an open invitation to an intellectual joust, ready or not. Such invitations were rare indeed, even in an academic setting, where the daily grind of teaching kept the average professor too busy to do anything but teach. Learning something new typically only occurred at conferences or while taking a sabbatical.

After establishing our love of books, Hap and I became fast friends. We often met at the student union building for coffee or a meal, or he joined me for bench therapy in the quad. Sometimes we even met for dinner. Had it been up to me, I would have had him in front of the classroom teaching one of his areas of expertise, which included history, philosophy, and theology. He was a rare bird, a walking encyclopedia of knowledge and wisdom. I was a better person because of him, and Simpson was a better place because of him

- - -

Hap finally spoke after we pulled onto the highway. "When I was younger, I remember every time I went to a wedding, someone would nudge me and say, 'You're next.' How come no one does that at funerals?"

I smiled as I stared ahead at the road.

"Seriously, though. I hope whoever does my eulogy says something like, 'He died doing what he loved: surprising tigers.'"

I let myself chuckle. "You're on a roll this morning, Hap."

"Well, you know what they say," he said with one hand on the wheel. "You can't have a funeral without fun."

"Ba-dum-bum! Don't quit your day job."

His eyes darted from the road to his rearview mirror and then back. "Funerals suck, don't they? At least you're not family, and nobody owes you any money. You're safe. Blood might be thicker than water, but money thins it out, don't you think?" The easygoing smile on his face disappeared. "Patrick, from what little you've told me about Sarah and your undergraduate days, I know this trip isn't a joyful one. She obviously meant a lot to you. When you get to Chicago, respect the process of burying someone, talk to a few people, pay your respects to the deceased, and then let it all go. You'll be lighter on your feet when you get back, trust me. Believe it or not, this trip of yours has done a number on me too. I have bones to bury when it comes to Chicago myself."

I turned toward him in the passenger seat, intrigued. "Yeah? I don't think you've ever mentioned Chicago in all the time I've known you." I checked my watch. "We've got a few minutes to kill before we reach the airport. Spill the beans, mister."

Hap narrowed his gaze at the flat road stretching toward the equally flat horizon. "I'm sure you've heard the expression 'shit happens.' Well, brother, in my case, it came in spades, and it was a beauty. I was visiting some relatives in Chicago who had moved up North from Mississippi a few years back. My mother couldn't travel. She had issues with her hip. So I was elected to take her place. I visited her sister and hung out with a few of my cousins.

"When I first got there, I was blown away. I'd never seen such tall buildings and so many people in one place. My cousin Harold just laughed at me. Said I looked like a deer in headlights. On my third day there, he suggested we take a road trip on the L, the elevated train, up to Wrigley Field to see the Cubs play. My auntie said we should stay on the South Side and watch a White Sox game instead. But since they were out of town for the week, it was the Cubs or no baseball game.

"Harold took the lead to get us back and forth. Said we should pool our money for the game and food and not worry about the fare for the L. Said he knew just how to manage getting to and from the game.

When we climbed the steps to the L, Harold looked around to see if anyone was looking and then told me to jump the stiles and calmly walk to the platform. I did as he said, and just like that, we were on our own way. After a dozen stops or so, we could see Wrigley Field in the distance. Harold, once again, told me to jump the stiles and move on like it was nothing. He said it would be easier to skip the fare since so many people would be coming and going. He suggested that I go first, and he would follow.

"The train slowed down, and we exited. Harold motioned for me to follow him and headed to the stiles. He slowed down and told me to go first. I approached the stiles and leaped. Harold was right behind me. Out of the blue, I heard someone yell, 'Stop, you two!' Then I heard Harold yell, 'Run for it!' I ran as fast as I could! But the police officer got a hold of us. He grabbed Harold's arm in one hand, tossed his billy club on the ground, and took my feet out from underneath me. I crashed to the cement, hitting my right knee, twisting my ankle, and slamming my forehead on the pavement. Man, I was in so much pain I blacked out! When I woke up, it had been several hours, and I was in my auntie's house on my back with ice packs on my head, ankle, and knee.

"My auntie tried her best to stop the pain and help me get my wits about me. Her son, on the other hand, was in his room under house arrest for having led her nephew astray. I asked my auntie for some aspirin, which she was able to provide, but a doctor was another story. She asked one of her friends who worked as a nurse's aide to come over and look at me. After checking my head wound and twisting my ankle to and fro, she gave her best medical opinion. She said I had a badly bruised forehead with a few raspberries, which would heal just nicely, and a twisted ankle, which needed to be elevated and iced to recover. But she said she was concerned about the knee. It was swollen and black and blue. She had never seen one so banged up before."

Hap switched on his turn signal and glided over into the passing lane to get past a slow-moving flatbed truck stacked with hay bales. "After another round of aspirin, my auntie made the dreaded phone call home to my mother. She was advised to let me heal and then put me on the train back to Mississippi. That she did, and I was home in three days on crutches with a normal ankle and a nice raspberry on my forehead. My issue with phone calls didn't end there. I had to call my football coach at Simpson and tell him about my messed-up knee."

I did a double take. "You played football at Simpson? I had no idea."

He nodded, and I could almost see his mind transporting him back to his glory days on the gridiron. "Yeah. Had a full-ride scholarship and everything."

"Amazing." I should my head in disbelief. "What position did you play?"

"Tailback. And sometimes I returned punts. The doctor told me and my mom that he needed to do follow-up exams and that I had to stay in bed for a spell until he could look at the x-rays. The results came back, and from what he could tell, there wasn't any major damage that could cripple me, but he told me that my football days were numbered. In his estimation, all it would take would be one bad fall or twist and my athletic career would be over."

I grimaced. "That's awful. So what happened?"

"All it took was the first game of my junior year. We were running a jet sweep to the weak side—I knew the play by heart—and I was racing to beat the linebacker who had containment when it happened. A defensive end snuck up behind me—had the perfect angle on me—and got me around the ankles and twisted me over. I heard a loud pop and knew it was the same knee torn to shreds.

"They carried me off the field, took me to the campus infirmary, and I lay there for what seemed like an eternity. Coach came to the infirmary, offered his condolences, and left. A few days later, on crutches once again, I went to his office to talk about my future. As I feared, Coach told me that my playing days were over at Simpson, but he convinced the administration that since I was in good academic standing, the athletic department would honor my scholarship until I graduated. Room and board, on the other hand, were on me."

"You must have been devastated."

He heaved a long sigh. "I was."

"But it sure seems like you took it in stride—pardon the pun."

Hap stared ahead at the road, a wistful smile playing at his lips. "Yeah, I did. Once I got back to the dorm, I called my mom to tell her the bad news about football and the good news about school. Between her sending money to cover the dorm and meals and me enrolling in a student work-study program, I managed to finish my junior year in good standing. For my senior year, my mom moved so she could be close to Simpson. Got a job as a childcare worker, bad hips and all, and I continued working at the library in the work-study program. By graduation, my mom had slowed down even more and was confined to staying at home. And by then, she didn't want to go back to Mississippi; Simpson College was her new home away from home."

"Wow," I said, still processing everything I'd just heard. "Any regrets?"

He shook his head defiantly. "Not at all. My mom was content to be with me at Simpson. She was as proud of my accomplishments in the classroom as she was of my success on the football field. In fact, I'd venture to say she was happy to see me secure a future that didn't depend on me throwing my body against three-hundred-pound linemen. Anyway, as far as I'm concerned, things happen for a reason. Who am I to wonder what could have been when it came to football?" He laughed aloud. "It wasn't like I had dreams of the NFL or anything related to that."

I thought for a moment. "How'd you get your nickname, anyway?"

"My grandma gave it to me," he said with a tight-lipped smile. "I was born due to happenstance in 1950 to an unwed mother who had a very pissed-off father, who happened to be ultraconservative and a Baptist minister."

"There's got to be more to the story than that."

He smiled again. "There is. I'll tell you another time. I promise."

Our exit appeared on the right, and soon we were easing into the passenger loading zone at the airport.

I got out, set my overnight back on the curb, and then leaned down to say goodbye to Hap. "I appreciate the ride," I said through the open window, "and the jokes and stories. You make great company, Hap."

"I know." He motioned with his eyes toward the entrance doors, which opened and closed automatically with each new wave of passengers. "When you get to Chicago, remember two things. First, keep an open mind and heart. And second, whatever it had to do with the past, bury it, let bygones be bygones, and move on."

Hap motioned for me to get out of the car and get going before I missed my flight. I grabbed my overnight bag and walked toward to airport departures without looking back. The doors opened, and I walked toward my gate, thinking only about Sarah and the letter that awaited.

8

BONES IN THE CLOSET

**"Let him who would move the world first
move himself."**
—Socrates

As the patchwork of flat farmland below shrank from view, Hap's sage advice rang in my ears. I spent the two-hour flight to Chicago thinking about burying the past once and for all. I knew full well I was not the first—nor would I be the last—to journey somewhere to pay their respects after the death of a loved one while doing some side business of their own. In my case, that meant burying the hatchet with Max and Sarah. The three of us had been pretty tight for three years. Sadly, things had gone sideways and had stayed that way for several decades.

I recognized Max as soon as I spotted him at the baggage claim. He had the same short stature and round glasses, but now he was balding on top, the tuft of hair on the back of his head resembling the mane of a horse.

"Wow!" I said as we clapped each other on the back. "You've hardly changed."

He gave me a quick once-over. "You too."

Outside of Christmas cards and the occasional phone call, we had done a lousy job of maintaining our friendship over the years. The spoils of youth had given way to the reality of adulthood for both of us. Life had gotten in the way, like it always does.

"Let's grab lunch before we go back to my place," Max suggested. "There's so much to talk about."

"Sounds good to me."

He drove us in his plush BMW to a classic diner near O'Hare, and after grabbing a corner booth in the well-lit joint, we sat down with a pair of menus.

"I had no idea about the letter," he said. "In fact, if it wasn't for the family lawyer contacting me about it, I would have left you out of the funeral arrangements altogether. My preference would have been to spare you from revisiting the past, considering how everything ended between you and Sarah. I was resolved to let sleeping dogs lie. Sarah's parents are both deceased. The only family to be at the funeral will be a cadre of siblings and cousins, plus a few friends."

"I appreciate it," I said, eyeing the menu.

A plump server with dyed red hair and too much makeup stopped at our table to take our orders. Max ordered a Reuben sandwich and French fries, and after pausing a moment to look over my options one last time, I did the same. I hadn't had corned beef, sauerkraut, and Swiss cheese on rye in a long time.

"You want fries with that or coleslaw?"

"Coleslaw," I said.

The waitress gave us a quick nod, took our menus, and disappeared into the kitchen, where we could hear her barking our orders to the chef in a singsong voice.

Max took a deep breath to compose himself and then picked up where he'd left off. "My wife doesn't know about my activism from our days at Baker. After I graduated, I went to Chicago and tried to lay low. I knew it was only a matter of time before I got drafted.

I was done with college, and nobody got deferments. I tried to stay active in the Students for a Democratic Society movement, but after the 1968 Democratic convention, Daley and the FBI started targeting protesters and any known SDS members living there. I bounced from low-level job to low-level job, trying to hide from the authorities and the draft board. At the suggestion of my parents, I applied to the law program at Rutgers University, and before I knew it, I was studying public advocacy law in New Jersey. By my second year there, I was dating a petite blond co-ed."

"Victoria?" I asked.

He stared wistfully out the window at the mostly empty parking lot. "Yeah. She was from a very Waspy family in Connecticut. Very conservative viewpoints about, well, just about everything. I was being led by my penis, not my mind. Out the window went public law, and in the front door came corporate law, courtesy of her father, who had mega connections in New York City and Philadelphia. I passed the bar, Victoria and I got married, and we had one kid on the way. As far as my in-laws were concerned, my past as an SDS activist, CORE member, and antiwar protester had never happened. I didn't mind. I wanted it to stay that way for Victoria's sake, not to mention our marriage and my Waspy in-laws."

Two pints of beer arrived before our sandwiches, and I took a long swig of mine. The plane ride had left me thirsty. More importantly, I was eager to take the edge off. I could feel myself growing tense as Max switched topics to the letter.

"As far as I can tell, the only reason the lawyer knew anything about you was because Sarah left detailed instructions on how to find you. She had heard through a mutual friend from Baker about my law school trek out East and how I ended up in Chicago. It wasn't hard to find me. I work for one of the biggest firms in Chicago. Like you, Sarah tried to bury the past after 1968. You had checked out in 1965, and I was the last link to Baker and our friendship. We met a few times in passing during the Chicago SDS rallies, but as the movement waned, new leadership took over and rebranded the movement into the Weather Underground. They took the SDS and radicalized and militarized it. Sadly for us, the common bond formed at Baker was broken. There was just no reason to stay in touch."

I nodded knowingly. "I get it. We all wanted to

move on. It was the best thing for everyone."

"Exactly. Nobody wanted to be associated with what the movement had become. The violence, the efforts to overthrow the government—it was too much. From what I remember, the Weather Underground formed at the University of Michigan and recruited disenchanted students at colleges and universities in the Midwest, Chicago in particular. Believe it or not, your name never came up in those meetings with Sarah. She'd probably heard the same news that I had: that you'd left Baker before your senior year and had taken a sabbatical year in Munich with your fiancée in tow."

"Technical University," I muttered.

"I never asked her what happened between you two and why she left Baker and never returned," Max said. "I figured it had to do with her father, because he was dead set against her going to Baker in the first place. The last I heard, she had transferred to the University of Chicago to study social work and English literature. With subjects like that, I figured she would likely end up in teaching or doing social work. After she graduated, she went into the Peace Corps and stayed in the service for over five years."

I sensed a black cloud descending on me. Instead of feeling liberated by Sarah's story—a story that had remained a mystery to me until now—I couldn't shake off a strange sense of doom. It seemed I had preferred not knowing to knowing.

After lunch, Max drove us to his house, an old brick Tudor on a stately tree-lined street in an old-money neighborhood. As the funeral service inched closer, I could feel my muscles tensing. I just wanted to get it over with it, but there was still the matter of Sarah's letter to resolve.

"This is Victoria," Max said as we entered the foyer.

Victoria, like their home, was well-kempt and still in her prime. She was dressed in dark slacks and a matching top, her blond hair arranged in an updo that looked simultaneously free-form and meticulously arranged. She shook my hand and introduced their two children, both adorable, before retreating with the kids to the living room.

As Max showed me to the guest room upstairs, I couldn't help but marvel at how much he had changed. Gone was the young college radical, replaced by an accomplished middle-aged professional. He had grown up—no small accomplishment in the modern world, certainly—and was nothing like the younger Max I had bonded with at Baker.

We ate a light supper that night, spent an hour or two reminiscing in Max's study, and then retired for the evening. It had been a long first day, but the funeral still loomed.

- - -

When we arrived at the funeral home the next morning, we learned that Sarah had insisted on a nontraditional viewing. In a stark departure from her Jewish upbringing, she had requested a secular ceremony: quick and easy. Outside of a few relatives wearing yarmulkes, the assemblage left no hint of Sarah's Jewish roots.

After two of Sarah's cousins greeted us warmly and thanked us for coming, we stepped inside the vestibule, where a table displayed dozens of photographs of Sarah during her Peace Corps days, her teaching and social work period in Chicago, and various family gatherings. The photos of Sarah from the late 1960s and 1970s hit me like a ton of bricks. She looked exactly as I had seen her last, with her long curly hair and wonderful smile. She stood tall in every photo, like Joan of Arc ready to do battle. And she didn't appear to be intimidated by those around her, including to my astonishment, well-known radicals like Bill Ayers. Over time, her youth had faded, replaced by a more refined and dignified countenance. She had aged well, and it showed.

As I moved through the receiving line, the worst was yet to come. Due to the cancer and at her request, she had asked to be cremated and have her ashes spread in a location only known to the family. My heart sank. There was no body to view. Leave it to Sarah, I thought, to have the last word on how she would be remembered. As I walked away, it hit me. I had been lucky enough to remember her as she was and, to some degree, how she had turned out.

After a respectful ceremony, during which family members told stories and a pianist played a few classical songs, the event drew to a close. We were asked to gather at her sister's house for a small get-together and share some food and companionship. Max and I obliged and made our way over to her sister's house in a middle-class neighborhood with tidy lawns and well-built homes. The whole affair lasted about two hours, and we celebrated with the family in a wholesome way. Her siblings recounted how Sarah had spoken fondly of her Baker days and her efforts with the SDS. I felt my heart swell when they said she had often mentioned her friendship with Max and me—no small thing, I told myself, considering I had been out of the picture after her departure from Baker.

Just before we left, Sarah's sister Norah approached me. She reminded me a bit of Sarah. She was shorter, and a little plain, but had that same sweet smile. "Can we talk a moment?"

"Of course."

She grabbed two glasses of wine and guided me outside to the back garden. The skies were leaden and the air crisp, but the autumn rain had held off all day thus far. After handing me a glass of chardonnay, she reached for my free hand and led me to a stone bench. We sat down and exchanged glances. I felt like I was staring at an older version of Sarah.

"Patrick," she said in a solemn voice, "I know what I'm about to tell you is extremely hard and hurtful. You have to trust me that what I'm about to say comes from Sarah."

I felt my stomach drop like an elevator and found myself closing my eyes, as if doing so might ward off whatever she was about to say. The last thing I had wanted to do was reopen old wounds.

"We spent quite a bit of time together at the hospital the past few years," Norah said. "We were always going back and forth to the doctor. The two of us were close for most of our lives, but there was a spell when there was another version of Sarah—one that was detached and angry and estranged from my family. While she was at Baker, there was deep resentment between Sarah and our parents, and I was drawn into it because I stood up for her.

"As you probably already know, my father was completely against her going to Baker. He wanted her to stay closer to home and go to the University of Chicago. She had been awarded a full ride, and it was her dream to study public advocacy and social work. Considering she had worked at the Hull House all through high school and had volunteered in several nonprofits, it only made sense for her to stay home and attend U of C. But she abruptly changed her mind and ended up at Baker. No one in the family, especially my father, knew what had happened. It came completely out of the blue the summer before she was to report as a first-year student at U of C." Norah paused to swirl her wine in its glass.

I wasn't sure I wanted to hear the rest.

"You probably don't know this," she said, "but Sarah's decision to go out West to Baker wasn't haphazard or something done on a whim. Something bad happened to her the summer before she was supposed to enroll at the University of Chicago." She paused again, this time to take a sip of the chardonnay, her hand trembling noticeably. "Patrick . . ." She grasped my hand. "Sarah was raped."

"Raped?" I repeated, barely able to choke out the word.

She nodded. "By a coworker. He offered to take her home after a fundraising function at one of the nonprofits she worked at. No charges were filed. How could they? There was alcohol served at the gala, and Sarah was seen drinking and dancing with the perpetrator. The whole thing was swept under the rug under the auspices of 'he said, she said.'" Tears welled up in her eyes as she paused to catch her breath. "I was the one who took her to the hospital and tried to get the police involved. Our father was livid at Sarah for drinking and dancing with someone who was older and in a supervisor role too. Sarah decided to go out West at the last second to put the whole sordid affair behind her. She needed to put time and distance between herself and the so-called justice system. She never told my parents what truly happened that night, and she swore me to secrecy." Norah gulped at her wine. "I know about your relationship with my sister while at Baker. When she let her guard down, she talked about the long walks you took, the talks you had, and the intellectual and spiritual chemistry you shared. I also know that she left you hanging in the summer of 1965. Please know that it wasn't easy for her. She was hurting. She locked away those days with you at Baker and held on to them until the end.

"She left you a long letter. I know because I wrote it for her as she dictated it to me. We tried to reach you in Decorah, but the first letter went unanswered. I helped Sarah write a second one, essentially saying the same thing, and through Max, we reached you. When you read it, a lot of what happened after she left will become clear, and hopefully, it'll put to rest what happened between the two of you. I want you to know that I'll be available to fill in any of the gaps, should the need arise." Norah took my hand, placed it in hers once again, and leaned over and kissed my cheek. She looked me straight in the eye. "Sarah never stopped loving you." With that, she stood up and walked back inside.

I remained on the bench, stunned and in silence, as all of the pain, suffering, and angst of Sarah's disappearance and subsequent silence came rushing back to me. But before I could wallow in the darkness, I suddenly felt a wave of peace that I'd never known. For the first time, I felt as if a weight had been lifted from my shoulders. I still had to read the letter, but for the moment, I was content to sit with my feelings. I was in no rush to process everything I'd just heard.

- - -

"I saw you talking to Norah in the garden," Max said as he drove us back to his place afterward. "How'd it go?"

I stared at a row of towering sycamores as we drove past them. They were mostly bare, their stout cream-colored trunks splotched with russet patches. "It went well. In a way, I felt like I was sitting with Sarah."

Max stared straight ahead. "I had the same feeling when we first met her. She has Sarah's smile."

We drove the rest of the way in silence, each of us

tapped out from the funeral. After spending the afternoon and evening talking about the old days and recounting names and stories from our days at Baker, we made plans for Max to drive me back to the airport the next morning.

And about ten hours later, after rolling to a stop at the passenger loading zone at O'Hare, Max handed me the letter. "Save it for when you get home. Find somewhere quiet to read it with no interruptions, and make sure you give yourself plenty of time. If you need to talk afterward, just give me a call. I'll be here." He offered a sad smile. "You might want to revisit some things."

"Thanks," I said and stuffed the envelope into my wool coat's inside pocket. "Don't be a stranger."

Sarah's funeral had brought our friendship back to life, and for that, I was feeling thankful.

9

THE LETTER

"Every action has its pleasures and its price."
—Socrates

As I sat waiting for my flight, I held the letter and stared at it. From what I could tell, it was only a few pages long. I brought it to my nose, hoping to catch a faint whiff of perfume or something, a final gift from Sarah. But nothing about it hinted at what was inside—or at what had occurred during the twenty-seven years since I had seen her. I returned the letter to my inside pocket and prepared to board.

Hap picked me up at the airport. He had once told

me I'd make a model prisoner because of my propensity to open up after the gentlest of prodding. And he had been right. I was a talker who sometimes didn't know when to shut up. I could hold an audience of one at bay for two hours answering one question or responding to one suggestion.

"Well," Hap said as we merged onto the highway, "how did it go? Did you find closure?"

I stared out the car window at the bare cornfields, unsure where to start. "The trip went well. I caught up with my old college friend Max. He's married now, a father, and a successful lawyer. Beautiful home. Far from the radical college kid I knew in my youth. He told me I should use the trip to get closure, just like you said." I motioned over my shoulder at my overnight bag in the back seat. "I didn't visit any bookstores, so my bag's no fuller than it was when I left. You probably consider that an incomplete trip."

"Nah," he said. "Your book-shopping fetish is the least of my concerns."

After a long pause, I spoke about the funeral. "It was a trip. They gathered a bunch of photos of Sarah and arranged them on a table. They showed the course of her life, from her youth to her last years." I shook my head in wonderment. "She aged like fine wine. Just as beautiful as I remembered her. Turns out she finished school in Chicago and then joined the Peace Corps. She worked at a nonprofit and then when into teaching."

"Interesting." Hap retorted.

"Get this," I said. "It turns out she also managed to play a part in making some history. She got herself mixed up with some radicals at the 1968 Democratic Convention that took place in Chicago."

Hap just shook his head and laughed aloud. "Sounds like you know how to pick 'em, Patrick."

I continued. "I did see some interesting photos that caught my eye. In one of them, she was standing on the steps of the federal courthouse protesting what happened with the Chicago Seven, and in another, she was with Bill Ayers, infamous member of the Weathermen Underground. There was a third that I wasn't sure about: a photo of Sarah with an older gentleman."

"Who do you think it was?"

I shrugged. "Just a guess, but he looked like Saul Alinsky, the American community activist and political theorist."

"Sounds like Sarah liked to hang out with some

interesting people," Hap quipped.

I didn't have to tell Hap that Alinsky had authored the playbook on radicalism in American politics, helped strategize the rise of the New Left on college campuses, and served as one of the leading advocates of Power in Chicago.

"I probably should have asked more questions at the funeral," I said. "I could have found out more. But there's a time and place for digging into someone's past, and a funeral isn't one of them. I guess I could have eavesdropped on a few more conversations to find out more."

No doubt, the letter in my coat pocket would fill in the gaps quite nicely. I told myself I could also follow up with Norah, if necessary.

A few minutes later, we pulled up to my house and sat in the driveway for a few minutes.

I caught sight of Gladys sneaking a peek at us through her drapes but ignored her. "Hap," I said, "I appreciate the lift. If you'll let me, I'd like to take you out for lunch at the student union next week."

He smiled. "Sure. I'm a cheap date."

I got out, opened the back door to retrieve my overnight bag, and then leaned into his window to say goodbye.

"Patrick," he said, "you can run from the past, but you can't hide from it. Whatever's in that letter, you have to let it go after you read it. Sounds like Sarah had a good head on her shoulders. Whatever she wrote to you must have been heartfelt and should bring closure." He offered a reassuring smile. "Love you, brother. Get those skeletons out of the closet and bury them in the backyard for good."

I went inside the house and had to ward off Socrates, who was thrilled to see me and, judging by his girth, had gained a pound or two in my brief absence, just like always. After unpacking my bag, I retired to my study. I set the letter on my desk and poured myself a scotch, and as I stared at the letter, I exhaled slowly through my mouth. I was ready to put to rest twenty-seven years of silence and confusion. While Socrates paced in the doorway, I opened the letter and began to read.

Dear Patrick,

It's not lost on me that this letter to you is long overdue. Please trust that a lot happened to me over the years that involve matters of the heart that aren't easily explained away. Nor are they to be understood in one letter. As you know by now, I had cancer, and it was terminal. As a part of my hospice care, I was encouraged to reach out to loved ones, past and present, and communicate to them in some fashion. Taking this advice to heart, I called a few loved ones, visited others, and wrote letters to those who were separated by miles, time, and circumstance.

As I write this letter, I want you to know that I have never forgotten you. Nor have I stopped loving you in more ways than one. As you know from your own experience in adult life, you can love someone for all the right reasons but not see it through. In our case, I want you to think back to our last conversation. We didn't exactly end on good terms, and it was quite apparent that we were on opposite sides when it came to the future. Even though we loved each other, the last three months of our spring semester at Baker were less than joyful. We argued constantly over how we were going to proceed with school and our activism in the SDS, CORE, and SNCC efforts. At the time, you were pulling back, and I wanted to go forward—so much so that I took a stand and asked you to man up. As harsh as it might have sounded at the time, I thought it was what was called for and needed. I saw you as the leader of something great, and you saw otherwise.

So . . . what happened after I left for the summer and you stayed at Baker to attend summer school to get caught up on your college credits? Lots, trust me. I returned home to a firestorm in Chicago. My father was still upset with me for having gone off to California instead of attending the University of Chicago on scholarship. The minute I got home, we started to fight. My mother and my sister Norah were at their wits' end wondering how to quiet us.

One night, my father approached me after I got home late from an SDS rally held at Northwestern University near my house. With raised voices and arms flying back and forth trying to enunciate our words and phrases, we ended up nose to nose at the top of the landing. I was on the top step making my way to my room when I tripped and fell backward down the stairs. I fell to the bottom with a thud. I was knocked out cold by the fall. I was taken to the hospital. When I awoke, I was in a lower body cast and fitted with an arm sling. I was out for over three days with a concussion. My mother and sister were there to greet me when I awoke. My mother filled in all the details. I had ruptured my spleen, fractured my hip in two places, and broken my fibula in my left leg.

To make matters worse, when they x-rayed me, the doctor asked my mother if I had been sexually active. To which my mother answered she had no clue. Just to be careful, the doctor did a pregnancy test, and it came back positive. Sadly, due to the nature of my injuries, the doctor advised my mother that I should have an abortion, since my uterus had been heavily damaged in the fall. Patrick, I want you to know I had no say in this decision. The decision was made for me. Any effort to get hold of you about this matter would have caused even greater harm, especially if you had tried to contact me or see me regarding this.

As you already know, your letters and your calls went unanswered in the summer and fall of '65 and continued into the next year. Due to health issues and poor relations at home, I elected to go back East to my aunt's house in New York City for a year. When I returned home to Chicago, I enrolled at the University of Chicago and studied social work and English literature. My studies became my only oasis for two years. I did stay active with the SDS, CORE, and

SNCC, but I did so without my father's knowledge. We had an agreement: I would go to the U of C, and I could do anything I wanted outside of class. And he wouldn't ask. And I wouldn't tell. Long story short, I was at the university for two years, from the fall of 1967 through the spring of 1969.

While at the University of Chicago, in addition to my normal studies, I continued to read up on Marxism, Leninism, and Communism. It wasn't lost on me that these were areas that you and I had shared a great interest in, discussed through and through, and debated late into the night. I thought about you quite a bit while I buried myself in my studies. Any thought of reaching out to you was considered moot, since you were studying in Germany and, from what I had heard, engaged. You have to know that your name in certain activist circles was still alive and well. I was constantly bombarded with, "Weren't you at Baker in '64 and '65?" "What happened to that Patrick Dolan guy?" "He was the face of the FSM and dropped off the face of the earth when things got thick and crazy." I managed to say something to the effect that you went to Germany to study physics and philosophy on sabbatical at the Technical University of Munich.

That usually put an end to the queries.

After some years passed, people stopped asking, and I managed to file the memory of you away. My life at U of C was relatively peaceful on the SDS, CORE, and SNCC front until the summer of 1968. Yes, the summer of 1968, when thousands of antiwar activists associated with various student activists groups rallied at the Democratic National Convention in Chicago to protest the war and their discontent with Hubert Humphrey's candidacy.

Patrick, I'm not trying to give you a history lesson; you know how this played out in Chicago. There were all kinds of riots and bloodshed involving protesters, police, and bystanders. I was one of the protesters that joined the ranks of the SDS under the leadership of Tom Hayden, a graduate from the University of Michigan. From what I understand, you and he were tight for a while, until you had a falling out over the direction of the FSM.

After the FSM stalled, Hayden was joined by Abbie Hoffman, Jerry Rubin, and Mark Rudd, who were verbal and visual shock jocks. However, things got crazy fast. The SDS splintered right before the convention, when organizations like the Youth

International Party (Yippies) and the National Mobilization Committee to End the War in Vietnam (MOBE) were mobilized and took over. When Hoffman and other radicals started to pitch another candidate, Pigasus the Immortal, on the steps of the Chicago Convention Center, we started to backpedal. We considered their actions counterproductive.

To make a long story short, I was at Lincoln Park helping organize the protesters from out-of-state when all hell broke loose. Mayor Daley ordered National Guard troops and police officers to harass patrons at the park, nearby hotels, and the convention amphitheater. He was hell-bent on backing his claim that Chicago was his city, and no long-haired freaks were going to ruin the Democratic National Convention.

When Daley instituted a curfew on Lincoln Park and had police and the National Guard clear it Sunday night, things dissolved quickly. I was knocked to the ground, clubbed, and gassed. I was later arrested and taken downtown. My sister and my mother bailed me out. My father had a lawyer talk to the arresting office and the court judge in hopes of having my charges lessened to simply disturbing the peace. Later, I made a court appearance and took a guilty plea. I agreed with the judge to follow through with my college plans in exchange for leniency. I was to continue my studies at the University of Chicago, stay out of trouble, graduate, and use my academic studies to prepare for a teaching career. All of this was true, of course, but on the judge's terms and not mine. In fact, at the time, I was still undecided about teaching, the Peace Corps, or going into nonprofit community organization.

So there you have it. I was active after I left Baker, and I saw it through to the end, or at least until I could no longer stomach the radicalism gone amok. I, instead, sought out other ways to help make the world a better place. I joined the Peace Corps and served for over six years. I traveled to Costa Rica, the Congo in Africa, and Ukraine. I came back to Chicago and assumed a career teaching English in high school for twelve years and finished my job working as a community organizer for two. When I got sick with cancer, I took a leave of absence and was unable to return. Outside of my career in nonprofit work and teaching, I didn't find love again. Nor did I really have any interest in having a family. I had concluded my *work and career was my spouse.*

Patrick, let me leave you with this. We met under the best of circumstances and enjoyed some really enriching, engaging, and memorable days at Baker. We shared more than some will ever find and enjoy— mind, body, and soul. For us, the divide in the road came, and we took different paths. However, even though we didn't end up together, we still managed to do our part to make the world a better place—you in teaching college and me with the Peace Corps, teaching, and community organizing. When you finish this letter, I ask that you burn it. Savor the words, thoughts, and memories, and let them go. Finish what you started, Patrick, and know that I'm proud of you, your work, and the path you took.

Love,
Sarah

I put the letter down, heaved a heavy sigh, and then read it again just to make sure I hadn't missed anything. Exhausted, I stepped outside, Socrates right on my heels, and walked to the fire pit in the backyard. As instructed, I burned the letter and started the process of putting it out of my mind for good. I did it without hesitation, because I knew if I kept reading it or held on to it for one more second, I'd start entertaining more questions. What had she meant by this or that? What hadn't she told me? What could have been, had I joined her in her activism? I sat on the patio for a bit, and Socrates took up a watchful position at my feet. He seemed to sense that I wasn't quite ready to reconnect, that something else required my attention. I couldn't help but wonder what had been in that first letter Sarah had sent me and how it had ended up lost. The ashes were still smoldering in the fire pit when I walked inside. It took all of my strength to not look back and save what was left of the letter. Hap's advice to bury the past rang in my ears loud and clear.

10

THAT "DAMN" FRAT DOG

**"We cannot live better than in seeking to
become better."**
—Socrates

After burning the letter, I sat in my study for a few
hours and graded papers. No matter how hard I tried,
I couldn't get the other letter—the one Sarah had
mailed but I had never received—out of my mind. I
gazed out the bay window facing the street. My favorite
maple tree's crimson leaves glowed in the waning
daylight. I reached for my mug full of coffee, and after
taking a sip, I nearly spit it out all over my desk as it hit

me. It was my dog, Socrates, duly named by the Simpson student body! Yes, my dog, that damned so-called frat dog, had taken the letter and buried it in the backyard somewhere.

Not long after I had taken him in, Socrates had developed an annoying habit of burying my mail, but before I get to that, I think it's best to start at the beginning.

- - -

One warm spring afternoon after finishing my final lecture of the day, I got into my prized '69 Volkswagen Beetle. But when I turned the key in the ignition, nothing happened.

"What the hell?" I muttered.

I tried it again, and once again, the engine refused to turn over. The car sat silent. Was it a dead battery? I checked the headlights and was relieved to see I hadn't left them on. I switched on the dome light but couldn't tell in the glaring afternoon sun if the dome was giving off light or if it was glowing at all. Frustrated, I threw open the door, got out, and popped the hood. I wasn't a motorhead, per se, but I knew my way around a car enough to give it a quick inspection. I tugged at the battery cables, neither of which showed any corrosion or sulfuric acid buildup, and each felt securely connected to its corresponding battery terminal. I surveyed the rest of the engine compartment. Nothing looked amiss.

"Damn it," I said as I shut the hood.

I stared up at the afternoon sun, which hung lazily in the Southwestern sky. The weather was mild, if a bit warm. I could have chased down Hap and asked for a ride home, but I only lived two and half miles from campus. Why not walk? I realized that when I got home, I could phone a towing company and have my VW towed to the auto shop. Having made my decision, I locked the car, removed the car key from my key chain, and hid it under the wheel well for the tow truck driver, and satchel in hand, started for home.

It didn't take long to cross the campus parking lot and join the sidewalk. I would take side streets where I could, but I would have to cross a couple of major intersections to get to my neighborhood, regardless of which route I took. As I walked, I took in the homes I passed and their neatly manicured gardens. Craftsman homes sat alongside bungalows and the occasional duplex or small apartment building. Pink tulips bloomed beneath saucer magnolia trees, also flowering pink.

I had covered about a half of a mile when I felt the presence of someone or something behind me. I turned around, and sure enough, there stood an Old English Sheepdog about ten or twelve feet away. It looked fairly healthy and probably weighed about ninety-five pounds or more, although its hair was matted and unkempt. It didn't appear aggressive. In fact, it seemed approachable. But I didn't have time to make friends. I wanted to get home and call the towing service, so I turned and continued on my way. The dog, unfortunately, continued to follow me. If I picked up the pace, it picked up the pace. If I slowed, it slowed. And if I stopped, it lay down on the sidewalk behind me, never more than ten or fifteen feet away.

My mind raced. Would it follow me all the way home? Would I have to call the animal shelter? The thought alone added to my anxiety. I didn't have time for this. My beloved VW was marooned at campus and needed towing. I hastened my pace once more, glancing over my shoulder with disgust at my shadow, who refused to sever the invisible tether between us. Was it a male or a female? It looked male to me, but I wasn't exactly an expert in sexing shaggy dogs.

Finally, I stopped and turned abruptly to face the dog. "Shoo!" I said, waving my arms for effect. "Go home!"

Undeterred, he lay down once again on the sidewalk. He was in no hurry, it seemed, and was willing to go at whatever pace I chose. The only thing he wouldn't do was give up.

When I reached the first of two busy intersections, I felt a wave of excitement followed by a pang of guilt. Here, I thought, I could put some distance between us, for certainly the noisy traffic would deter him. But what if he followed me into the busy street or, worse, got hit by a car? I gritted my teeth and raced across a crosswalk to the other side, determined not to look back. When I didn't hear the sound of a honking horn or screeching tires, I allowed myself to entertain the hope that I'd left the dog stranded on the other side of the street. I continued another block and didn't look over my shoulder until I had turned onto a quiet side street.

He was still on my tail, a goofy grin on his face, his tongue lolling from the side of his mouth.

"Go away!" I said, not bothering to hide my exasperation. "Leave me be; I don't have time for this."

When we reached the last busy intersection before my neighborhood, we repeated the same exercise. I darted across the street, too afraid to look back at the mayhem that might occur on my heels, but not so afraid that I didn't relish the opportunity to escape my tormentor, and he somehow survived the gauntlet of traffic and remained on my tail, the caboose to my engine.

Once on my property, I bounded up the steps to my front porch, unlocked the front door, and slipped inside without looking back.

"Do not let the dog in," I muttered to myself, "or you'll never get rid of him."

I went about my business, calling the repair shop, making dinner, and grading papers in my study. Every once in a while, I hazarded a peek out the bay window, and each time, I saw the dog lying on the sidewalk in front of my house. How long could he remain lodged there? Surely, I told myself, he would give up and go home. But every time I looked up, I saw that he remained at his station.

He was still there when I turned off the light in my study, when I brushed my teeth, and when I crawled into bed.

The first thing I did the next morning was march to the front window and peer outside. To my great dismay, there he was, lying beneath a broad-canopied maple tree in the planting strip. He seemed lonely but somehow content, as if he'd found his forever home. His determination was admirable, I told myself, if misplaced.

While sitting down to a breakfast of black coffee, toast, and orange juice, I came up with what seemed like a simple course of action. My car was in the shop and cabs were notoriously hard to get in the morning, so I decided to walk to school in the mild spring air. The dog would follow me back and, if all went to plan, become reacquainted with the familiar scents of wherever he came from and follow his nose home.

Everything went as planned until I reached campus and saw that the dog was still shadowing me.

Shouldn't he have found his way home by now?

I gave him one more glance over the shoulder before disappearing inside the department office building. Fifteen minutes later, and much to my chagrin, he was waiting for me outside when I left for my first lecture.

Once again, I found myself muttering as I hurried

past him, "I don't have time for this."

I stormed toward my class in Hickock Hall, the dog still on my heels, and stepped inside without looking back.

"Is that your dog?" one of my students asked.

"Did you get a new dog, Professor?" another chimed in.

"No," I said, waving off the chorus of questions. "I don't know who that dog belongs to, but I can assure you that it's not mine."

I dove into my lecture, determined to ignore the problem, but every time I glanced outside, I spotted students stopping to pet the dog and offer it food. Soon a young man arrived with a yellow tennis ball and was playing fetch with the dog. It seemed the dog, the students, and I were one big happy family.

An hour later, students at my second class were asking about "my" dog, which apparently had a name.

"When do we get to meet Socrates?" a young woman asked from the front row. "And is it true that we can earn extra credit if we take him for a walk around the quad?"

My head spun. "What? Where do you hear that?"

"Everyone's talking about it," she said with a

shrug.

Several other students murmured in unison, drowning out each other's comments.

I raised my hand to silence the classroom. "All right. Listen carefully to me, everyone. That's not my dog. I don't know who it belongs to. And I'm not handing out extra credit for anything related to it. Okay?"

Several faces fell in disappointment, but some students appeared skeptical, as if the rumors churning through campus were more believable than my proclamation on the subject. It took everything I had to keep everyone focused on the lecture, and afterward, having reached my wits' end, I retreated to my office and dialed the number to security on my phone.

"Campus police," the desk sergeant answered in an abrupt tone.

"Yes," I said, suddenly feeling thankful I wasn't experiencing a serious emergency. "There's a dog on campus. It followed me to my class."

"Professor Dolan? We heard about your dog. Please don't bring Socrates to school again."

I shook my head angrily. "It's not my dog."

"I don't care who's dog it is," he snapped. "I'm the

one who has to deal with students afraid of some dog on the loose. Just because you're a professor doesn't mean you get a free pass to let some dog on campus."

"Look, Officer, as I said, the dog's not mine. I have no idea where it came from. It just followed me to school."

"Can't imagine anyone but a philosophy professor naming his dog Socrates," the cop chimed in.

"Excuse me?" My eyes widened in disbelief. "I'm not going to say it again. The dog. Isn't. Mine. Got it?"

"If you say so, Professor," he said in a dismissive tone that suggested he still didn't believe me. "We're too busy to deal with this kind of problem. I would suggest you bring the dog to the SPCA and have it impounded."

"Fine!" I said and slammed the phone into its cradle before the desk sergeant could respond.

I couldn't believe he was making the dog my problem. But I did as he suggested and called the animal shelter. Later that same day, a team from the shelter arrived and hauled this misguided dog named Socrates away.

For the next several days, my suddenly crestfallen students harassed me for my apparent cruelty to the dog. After a week had passed, I called the shelter to get an update on Socrates.

"Is this Professor Dolan?" asked the young woman who answered the phone.

"How'd you know?"

"I'm a part-time student at Simpson. We haven't seen Socrates for over five days. He got out somehow during feeding time and hasn't been seen since."

"You're kidding."

"I wish I was."

"Well, I guess that's it then," I said, unsure of what else to say.

The young woman seemed surprised my resigned tone. "Don't worry, Professor Dolan. We'll find your dog."

"He's not my—" I stopped myself, thanked her for her time, and hung up.

By now my VW was once again humming along, the proud owner of a new battery with a five-year warranty. When I pulled into the faculty parking lot the next morning, I took a deep breath, certain the Socrates saga was behind me. My sense of ease lasted until I spotted the first of dozens of "missing dog" flyers posted all over campus. A reward had been posted to "help find Professor Dolan's lost dog, Socrates." Hap told me over a cup of coffee later that morning that the amount had already been bumped up to $500.

"This is nuts," I said.

He laughed but offered no consoling words. If the whole thing was a joke, the joke was on me, and Hap was enjoying himself.

I paid several indifferent students to tear down the lost-dog signs, but more appeared the next day. I was fighting a losing battle.

That weekend, while reading the Sunday morning paper, I heard a knock at my front door. I tightened my bathrobe and shuffled to the door, only to find Socrates waiting for me on the porch. He was sporting a new bright-red collar and leash, the latter of which had been tied off to the porch railing. A note had been secured to a plastic bag that had been left beside the front door.

"What the—"

A jacked-up Honda with a noisy muffler sped down the street. I could almost hear the occupants laughing inside.

Despondent, with no fight left in me, I took Socrates and the plastic bag inside, sat down on the stairs near the entryway, and opened the note.

Dear Professor Dolan,

We, the fraternity brothers at Delta Tau Chi, would like to apologize for getting Socrates back to you so late. We found him wandering around campus on Thursday afternoon and took him home to clean him up and feed him. We heard, after the fact, that he was your dog, so we were relieved to know he was a Simpson guy.

However, before we could return him to you, we got caught up in getting ready for Simpson's homecoming. In fact, we decided at the last second to have Socrates serve as the fraternity mascot on our float. After the homecoming game against Cornell, we had a party, and things got a little out of hand. We were doing a beer keg and shots at the frat, and it turns out that Socrates is quite the partier. Who knew a dog would be into shots of tequila? The sorority girls from Delta Delta Delta were quite taken with him as well. Needless to say, we had quite the time with Socrates. He was a little hungover on Saturday morning, so we elected to have him stay over and sober up.

Again, sorry for the delay getting him back to you. In the bag, you'll find some goodies for Socrates, a fraternity sweater, a shot glass, and a paddle with his name on it.

Todd Pennington
Fraternity Chair, Delta Tau Chi
Simpson College

I put the letter down just as the phone rang.

Eying Socrates as I walked, I stepped into the living room and grabbed the phone off the end table. "Hello?"

"Professor Dolan," someone said on the other end of the line. "It's Beau Chesterman."

I rolled my eyes. Beau Chesterman, or Chesty Bowman as some faculty members liked to call him when he was out of earshot, was the Simpson College provost and the most pretentious man I'd ever met. Every word he spoke dripped with Ivy League pretension. His letters to the faculty were laden with twenty-dollar words. One had to use a dictionary to figure out what they meant or what language he spoke. How he had ended up in Iowa was anyone's guess.

"Ah, Mr. Chesterman," I said. "How can I help you?"

"Well," Beau said, pausing to clear his voice, "first

of all, I wanted to make sure you got your dog back safely."

"He's not my—" Once again, I cut myself off. Everyone at Simpson College seemed to think Socrates was my dog. It was a fait accompli. "Yes, he's fine."

"Splendid. Listen, I don't know if you're aware of this or not, but your dog spent the weekend with the Delta Tau Chi fraternity."

I stifled a laugh. "I'm aware."

"Well, you should know that I gave the fraternity a stern talking to. They've promised it won't happen again."

"That's fine," I said with a shrug.

"You see . . ." The provost seemed unsure how to proceed. "I just wanted to make sure that . . . you . . . Well, I'd hate to see you press charges or anything against the fraternity."

Now I was laughing out loud. "What for? Dognapping? Don't worry about it, Chester—I mean Beau. The boys from the fraternity dropped Socrates off with a letter that explained everything. The dog seems fine."

"I appreciate you letting it slide," he said. The provost followed up by saying, "Let's just say we will let bygones be bygones."

Shaking my head, I let out a big sigh. Even as frustrated as I was about the dog. I had no inclination to explain how I had met Socrates or how I had tried to ditch him and then, failing at that, pawn him off on the animal shelter.

By the time I got off the phone with Beau Chesterman, Socrates was fast asleep and snoring away on the couch in the living room.

- - -

The next morning, after letting Socrates out to pee on the backyard shrubbery, I opened the front door to retrieve the morning paper. Upon folding it under my arm, I took it, along with a cup of coffee, to the back deck to join Socrates. Once seated, I unfolded the paper and was astonished but somehow not surprised to see a photo of the Delta Tau Chi float from the Simpson homecoming parade. However, what I did not expect to see was my so-called new dog proud as a peacock and sitting like a king upon his thrown, traveling before his subjects. In the front seat of the float was that "damn frat" dog Socrates. All I could do was shake my head in disbelief and finally relent to a feeling of pride.

The caption beneath the photo read:

Socrates steals the show at the Simpson College homecoming parade.

It turned out the dog had been awarded the homecoming spirit trophy by the Simpson student body and nominated to be the homecoming grand marshal for next year's parade.

I put down the paper and acknowledged Socrates, who was sitting expectantly at my feet. All I could do was laugh at it all. I looked at Socrates and back to the newspaper. Just as I was about to say something, he stuck out his paw and barked at me. "I give up. You can stay."

So, there you have it. This is how I was adopted by a stray dog that was duly named Socrates and became a favorite of the Simpson College student body.

Socrates had only been with me for a month or two when my mail started disappearing on occasion. My mail carrier liked Socrates and often gave him a treat through the mail slot at the bottom of my front door. As soon as Socrates had the treat in his mouth, he would take it along with my mail through the recently installed doggie door in the back door and then bury it in the backyard. I didn't figure out what was going on until I mowed the lawn one sunny Saturday and noticed a freshly dug hole with an envelope partially sticking out of it. From that day on, I asked the mail carrier to leave my mail on the front porch swing for safekeeping.

The new practice worked well—unless my mail carrier was sick or on vacation and the substitute carrier dropped the mail through the slot. Fortunately, I knew where to look if an important bill or letter failed to arrive.

- - -

I thought about Sarah's lost letter as I stared outside. I could dig up the entire backyard, searching in vain for a letter that for all I knew had decomposed by now, or I could let it go. What chafed the most, I realized, was the fact that Sarah had lived long enough to dictate another letter—the letter I had actually read. Had I received her first missive, it was possible, maybe even probable, that the letter could have led to a lengthy and satisfying phone conversation. Maybe I would have even paid a visit to Chicago. Hearing her voice one last time, seeing her in the flesh—the idea haunted me. What else would she have told me? What could she have conveyed over the phone or in person that she had been unable to in her letter? Fortunately for me, the person who had helped her write the second letter was still alive and had offered to help me fill in the blanks if needed.

11

9:00 A.M. PHILOSOPHY #2

"Falling down is not a failure. Failure comes when you stay where you have fallen."
—Socrates

On my first day back with my philosophy class since returning from my trip to Chicago, I began my lecture by writing two questions on the blackboard. The chalk broke between my fingers as I wrote, but I managed to finish with the nub remaining in my right hand:

Who is Socrates?
What is the relationship between his call for

justice for Athenian youths and the question, "Why?"

As a rule, I liked to start each lecture with a little review just to see what had stuck and what had not. The approach had a twofold purpose: It gave the students a chance to revisit the topic and put it into their own words as they demonstrated what they knew in relation to the material, and it allowed me to discern how much they had retained from the previous lecture.

By the looks on their faces, I might as well have asked them to give blood.

Slowly, one hand went up. Denise Tate, seated in the back row, answered sheepishly, "Socrates was a Greek philosopher who lived around 399 BC and got into trouble asking 'big' questions about life and its relationship to moral and ethical traditions that form the basis of Western philosophy."

I was impressed. The reserved freshman was becoming more assertive every day. "Denise, that's a great start. Does anybody want to add to this?"

Roger Warren jumped into the discussion from the front row. "Socrates isn't known to have left anything written down. What we know of his life and teachings comes from the writings of his two prized students, Plato and Xenophon. These writings are called Socratic dialogues, which eventually got him into trouble with the Athenian authorities on charges that he was corrupting Athenian youths. Sadly, he was charged, tried, and convicted. He was sentenced to death. Socrates died by drinking hemlock." Roger paused to gather his thoughts. "It's not much of a stretch to say that your line of questioning in our class is based on Socrates's teachings. It's called the Socratic method: succinct questions that lead to short answers in order to show our ignorance and find wisdom along the way."

"Well done," I said, impressed that Roger was taking the lesson seriously. He was normally more prone to jesting. "Denise, you're mostly correct about Socrates and his impact on Western philosophy. His work served as the basis for using rationalism and ethics to ask big questions, look for abstract meaning, and relate it to virtues like knowledge, courage, and justice. And yes, Roger, you're also correct. Socrates claimed that all of us are ignorant in some fashion and that our search for knowledge leads to wisdom, which leaves us less ignorant. As far as the trial goes, he was found guilty of corrupting Athenian youths and leading them to a state of impiety. In other words, he was accused of encouraging Athenian youths to worship false gods and ignore practices and traditions of the state religion. More importantly, Socrates was also critical of Athenian leaders, namely democrats and the oligarchs. In his defense, he argued that gods do terrible things just like humans do. He also argued that each human being has an inner voice that isn't divine in origin. To this extent, he also questioned the existence of many gods and argued that there is only one god. On the charge of corruption, he replied that in corrupting others, the corrupter runs the risk of becoming corrupted themselves; hence, it's illogical and undesirable to do so."

We spent the next forty-five minutes diving deeper into the text. I ended class with another assignment, due next week.

"I've left a reading list in the library of scholarly articles on Socratic dialogues," I told the class. "I want each of you to take an article listed in the folder provided, put your name next to the academic article, read it, and talk about it in the next class. To be more explicit, I've identified the scholars as coming from three eras: the Renaissance, the Enlightenment, and the Modern Age." I remembered Hap's note, still fresh in my memory as though I'd read it only a day prior, and elaborated further. "You might recognize some of these names: Leonardo Bruni, Giannozzo Manetti, Marsilio Ficino, Hegel, Voltaire, and Friedrich Nietzsche."

Denise raised her hand as the clock on the far wall ticked off the last few seconds of class.

I nodded in her direction. "Yes?"

"Did you make the right number of copies this time, Professor? I don't want to have to battle my classmates for the readings like I did last time."

"Yes, I did. Thank you for bringing that up again, Denise."

I reminded my students these printed readings were selected to keep the costs down. There was no sense of having them buy a textbook they probably would not read. More importantly, there were enough copies for all to partake. A few of my students chuckled, but most of them, judging by the hangdog expressions on their faces, couldn't believe that I'd suggested going to the library once again to secure readings related to Socrates and the scholars who criticized his teachings and their impact over the centuries.

"You'll have the rest of the week to complete your readings," I said, which seemed to lighten the mood. "The accompanying exam will be open notes."

Just when I thought I was home free to dismiss them, Mark Birch raised his hand.

"Yes, Mr. Birch."

Mark furrowed his brow. "Are we ever going to return to your quest to challenge the status quo and what relationship it had to Socrates's efforts in 399 BC?"

I cocked my head slightly, surprised by the question. "Since you made the effort to correlate it to Socrates's efforts, I'll see what I can do. There's no sense in studying the past if you're not going to relate it to the present—or near present."

As much as I didn't want to admit it, Mark had me dead to rights. Young people served as agents of change, however incremental. I owed it to my students to make my lessons and related readings as relevant as possible. I also owed them the opportunity to consider my pedagogical philosophy. That, in my opinion, was what good teachers did: They made learning relevant, and they supported that quest by helping to dispel ignorance and impart the importance of critical thinking, reading, and writing along the way. I knew it was a lofty goal, but someone had to do it. I often told my students that while they toiled with their class assignments late at night, they could hate me now and love me later.

On the way to my office, I spotted Hap in the courtyard. He was armed with a long black umbrella but had yet to open it. For the moment, the forecasted rain had yet to begin falling.

"You recovered from your trip?" he asked.

"More or less," I said. "The downfalls of going out of town in the middle of the semester are trying to find time to unpack your bag, wash dirty laundry, and take care of whatever chores you put off before leaving."

"At least you live alone," Hap said, raising an eyebrow. "If you don't count that celebrated and highly esteemed dog of yours."

I laughed. "True enough. It's nice that I don't have to answer to anyone but myself. But I still have to keep the place clean and tidy. You never know when a colleague or friend might drop by."

"There's no use trying to hide your domestic shortcomings," Hap said. "It's a lost cause. Besides, those of us who know and appreciate you aren't inspecting your shelves for dust when we visit."

"No," I said, "usually you're too busy eyeing my collection of books."

"Don't forget the excellent stock of wine," Hap said, "and your record collection."

I felt a tiny surge of pride. I had an eclectic music library that usually fit the bill, whether I was hosting a small gathering or a full-blown party. "Anything new at the library?"

"Yes, as a matter of fact," Hap said. "We got a huge shipment of new books last week, but they won't be on the shelves for a while longer. It takes us a while to enter them into the system."

I felt a drop of rain and gazed up at the foreboding sky. "Well, I better keep moving. Looks like it's about to unload."

Hap readied his umbrella and nodded. "See you later, Patrick."

As I hurried across the quad, I reflected on how lucky I was to teach philosophy *and* physics. Both showed how the world operated—one on the physical level, the other on the metaphysical plane. To accomplish this wonderful feat, I got to hang out with Sir Isaac Newton, Socrates, Plato, Aristotle, and a host of others. Perhaps I didn't have too much to show for the wonderful deal I had struck with my father thirty years earlier, but everything had worked out well for me.

If I had a complaint, it was that I wished my philosophy students read more. They often seemed overwhelmed by the basics, but I wanted them to know that a whole world of ideas and exploration awaited them. They just needed that little spark of curiosity to guide them.

By the time I reached my office, it had begun to rain outside in earnest. I gathered some books and papers to be graded and then checked my answering machine. The first message was from my department chair. The second was from Norah. I felt my heart skip a beat at the sound of her voice.

"Hey, Patrick. It's Norah. I just wanted to make sure you're doing okay. If you need to talk, I'm here."

I wrote her number on a sticky note and slipped it into my pocket for safekeeping. I had mixed emotions about reaching out to Norah, considering I had burned the letter and all. But it seemed I still had more questions than answers.

When I got home from Simpson, I spotted a shovel

on the front porch. Attached was a note from Hap.

Dear Patrick,

I'm loaning you my prized shovel. Be sure to use it in the backyard when you're burying the past. If you need any guidance on how to do so, please call me.

Regards,

Hap

All I could do was shake my head in amazement. "He's always one step ahead of me," I muttered. It was likely he had already dropped off the shovel by the time we spoke earlier in the quad, but he hadn't let on. I hadn't told him I had burned the letter, but even if I had, he no doubt would have sensed that I was still holding on to something that needed burying.

I looked up from the shovel with a big smile on my face—one that even the sight of Gladys glaring at me from her front porch couldn't erase. I carried the shovel inside and found Socrates waiting for me in the entryway.

"You ready for a walk in the rain, big guy?"

He smiled like a doofus and wagged his tail.

Things could have worked out differently with

Sarah, I thought as I retrieved Socrates's leash from the coat rack, but then I wouldn't have led the life I had lived. For the most part, I felt like I was exactly where I was supposed to be, but I couldn't shake the feeling that Sarah still had more to tell me. What exactly remained to be seen and heard. The closure I had been seeking from my trip to Chicago was wavering. The shovel on the front porch did not help.

12

UNIVERSITY BLUES

"Understanding the question is half the answer."
—Socrates

The rain was still coming down after my neighborhood walk with Socrates. After shaking off my umbrella in the mudroom, I grabbed Hap's shovel, a sturdy symbol of his friendship, and carried it to the backyard. With Socrates at my side, I turned over a tuft of soil, lodged the shovel back into the ground, and then retired with a glass of merlot to the back porch. Socrates sat at my feet as we listened to the autumn rain. It was a little chilly out, but thankfully I had a wool blanket handy and was able to make myself comfortable.

Even though I had burned the letter from Sarah earlier, the words on the page were still fresh in my mind. They still haunted me. I couldn't help but ponder what she had written about our love affair, our breakup, and our activism and protests at Baker University from 1962 to 1965. I was grateful that the letter had cleared up so much of the mystery between the two of us, including how, some twenty-seven years ago, we had ended up apart.

As I stared at the glass of merlot in my hand, peering into its dark-plum depths, I sensed a feeling of restlessness overtaking me. I was wrestling with forces within and beyond me, still trying to understand my life's trajectory. Even though I had dropped out of the Free Speech Movement and moved on from Baker in the spring of 1965, my education had continued. I tried to bury my past by accepting an appointment as an exchange student at the Technical University of Munich in Germany as a physics and philosophy major. However, I couldn't help but think that my academic career as a college student and eventually an instructor was still being guided by my efforts to balance the physical and philosophical worlds. No easy task since they mixed like oil and water. Trying to separate the two was pointless. I always tried to put myself into the shoes of my students, which meant attempting to answer the immortal questions, "What's the point of this guy's lecture?" and "What does it all mean in the grand scheme of things?" And, yes, not too far off in the distance, I could still hear my father's voice. "How is this degree going to earn you a living?"

As much as I would have liked to blame myself for my current predicament, I knew that some of the blame rested on Socrates's shoulders. By seeking truth as a scholar, an instructor, and a fellow human being, I was charged with telling the truth, even if it meant exploring my personal history in the tumultuous sixties. How could someone not get involved when presented with information that questioned the essence of being a human and challenged the listener to denote his or her role in society? Who was I as a human being? And what had I been attempting to accomplish when I isolated myself from society and thrust myself into university life to study ethics and morality?

I left the comfort of the back porch long enough to

retrieve Hap's shovel in the rain and then found a rag inside to clean it off and dry it.

- - -

While the classroom began to fill up before my next philosophy lecture, I spotted Alex Keaton, a budding young journalist, in the back row. Armed with a reporter's notebook and a pair of pens, the bespectacled young man wore khaki pants, a white oxford shirt, and a bow tie. His short dark hair was neat and tidy—just like the rest of his appearance. He obviously took his role seriously.

With the encouragement of my department head, I had granted the young man access to my class so he could sit in on a lecture and write an article for the school newspaper. I was told it would not only go a long way toward helping him finish his assigned story but also increase enrollment in my classes. "Simpson students are passing up humanities classes in droves," my chair had reminded me. "A little personality in the classroom could shore up the numbers."

After the last of the students filled the remaining seats, we resumed our discussion of Socrates and the Socratic method. We made steady progress, discussing not only the great philosopher but the historical elements that played a significant role in his story.

Then, about a half hour into the lecture, I put down my chalk, dusted off my hands, and turned to face the students. "Okay," I said. "For the rest of our time today, we're going to do something a little different. A few lectures ago, I shared some personal details about my years as a student and talked about how it related to the course material. Some of you have been indicating you'd like to hear more about my story, so for the rest of this lecture, I'm going to temporarily abandon the syllabus and focus on 'real life' lessons and how they fit into the philosophical tradition. You don't need to take notes. None of this will end up on a test. This is just for your edification."

The students' faces brightened, and I watched as several stashed their notebooks and pens in their backpacks and leaned back in their seats in anticipation. Storytelling, I sometimes forgot, was a powerful tool, especially when it was detached from academic expectations.

I took a deep breath and exhaled slowly to focus my mind. From the back of the classroom, I heard a loud voice boom, "All hail the Baker Storm. Our 1960s radical has returned. Let it rip professor."

All I could do was shake my head and smile. "One of the reasons I climbed up on that campus police car and later stood on the steps of Westlake Hall at Baker University in the fall of 1964 was that I realized that the university was turning into a diploma factory that churned out docile workers, trained and brainwashed for the corporate world. All you had to do was look at the student protests of the 1920s and 1930s. Those students were in the throes of the Great Depression, yet they found the courage to question why they were being asked to study engineering and business. My generation was picking up where they had left off. Our fight three decades ago was centered on civil rights, free speech, and the right to assemble peacefully on campus and share our concerns."

I paused. The students seemed interested in what I had to say.

It was time to introduce the name of a philosopher that I hoped most of my students would recognize. "Immanuel Kant wrote that in order to be moral, you have to think and act morally, even when no one's looking. Kant's charge to humankind was 'You always treat humanity as an end and never as a means to an end. You are to act not because you want to act but because you *ought* to act.' So that's what tens of thousands of my peers did in the early 1960s. Many continued for a decade or more."

I stared down at my notes, which I had cobbled together the night before in my study, and quickly realized I didn't need them. I had already gone off script. It was time to follow my muse and trust that I would arrive at the points I hoped to make. I folded the notes and stuffed them into the inside pocket of my tweed jacket.

"One of the joys of teaching physics and philosophy is the independence that it fosters. I get to step out of the mainstream curriculum at the modern university and tackle some age-old questions that have been beguiling learned minds for anywhere from a few decades to several centuries. Sadly, the evolution of colleges and universities of late has made teaching humanities courses an anachronistic endeavor. The field of physics is safe for the most part, since it utilizes a plethora of math and theorems. But it's the field of philosophy and its fate and role in society that worries me. Some argue it's on its way out, sooner or later.

"Colleges and universities have evolved dramatically over the past three hundred years in the

United States. Once designed to train ministers for the clergy, they now educate engineers and businesspeople for the marketplace. They develop astrophysicists and biologists for God knows what. Lately, as we approach the twenty-first century, all I've been hearing about is the importance of STEM studies: science, technology, math, and engineering. Never mind that this props up the very thing Eisenhower warned us about in his farewell speech to the nation in 1960: the military-industrial complex. The embrace of technology over humanity certainly isn't the path that I would have expected to take when I was your age."

I took a moment to gauge the reaction of my students. Were they making any connections? Could they sense where I was taking them? Mark Birch had a hand on his chin and stared at me expectantly, like he was waiting for me to deliver a punch line of sorts—or at least circle back to my biography. It was clear he and his classmates were more curious about my experiences than my opinion.

The aspiring journalist in the back raised his hand.

"Class," I said, "we have a visitor today from the journalism department. This is Alex Keaton." I nodded to the young man. "Do you have a question, Mr.

Keaton?"

"Yes." Far from being intimidated by my introduction, he seemed empowered by the many eyes staring in his direction. "What do you think is the future of humanities at the modern university?"

I knew I should answer cautiously. I had already taken the class on a detour. Now I was being asked to speak on the record. But something about the challenge emboldened me. How far could I take academic freedom? I was eager to find out. "When you get down to it," I said, "the study of humanities is screwed."

Several of my students drew back in surprise. A few gasped. One or two giggled.

"Never mind that it was the humanities that brought us the Renaissance and the Enlightenment in both Europe and America," I continued. "If you want to point fingers at the demise of the humanities, look at who is running the show these days. Our administrators' cattle-herd our students in and out of class in a timely fashion to meet the needs of a capitalistic society bent on elevating STEM courses over everything else, all in the name of looking out for the welfare of the student. In one ear, I hear from parents demanding that their children have something to show for four years of academic sweat and toil, and in the other, I hear from regional and national leaders who want to prepare students to enter the professional ranks ready, willing, and able to tackle national problems and create engines of economic growth."

Several students clapped and hooted.

"Way to go, Professor!" Mark shouted. "Let the suits have it. Keep it going. This is good stuff."

By now, I had completely forgotten the student journalist. I paced the front of the classroom, searching my students' faces, hoping to make eye contact and speak directly to their hearts. "As your instructor and a representative of this university, I'm charged by the university mission statement and academic goals to promote, foster, and expect critical thinking, reading, and writing at the highest level, regardless of the field of study. This should be the goal of anyone pursuing a four-year college degree. But forces outside the university undermine everything I do. The world—corporations, to be more specific—dictates what skills and talents are required, not to mention what degrees are worth the paper they're printed on. They have the assistance of local, state, and federal governments, of course. The days of coming to the university to study philosophy, English literature, or any of the soft sciences for the sake of higher truths and personal edification are over, as far as I'm concerned. Rarely do we see students rally around the flag in the name of social and economic justice, as my peers and I did in the 1960s and early 1970s. Sad to say, the university is no longer the epicenter of protests for a new moral high ground that endeavors to address the plight of the poor and disenfranchised."

The students fell silent. Were they feeling inspired? Chastised? Confused? I wasn't even sure how *I* felt. It was a relief to be real with them, to tell them exactly how I felt about the state of academia. But I also felt a strange sense of guilt, as if I had just handed them a burden that belonged to my generation, not theirs.

I looked at the clock. We still had time left. But I couldn't imagine resuming anything resembling a normal lesson. In retrospect, I could and should have opened the floor to my students. An informal Q&A likely would have proved beneficial. If nothing else, it would have given everyone a moment to process some of what I had just said. But having exposed the dark path modern colleges and universities were following, I felt compelled to pull back. Suddenly, after sharing far too much, I was feeling circumspect.

"I know we have a few minutes remaining," I said, "but I want to leave this right here for the moment. Take some time to let everything I said sink in. We can talk more in the coming days. In the meantime, have a great weekend."

I dismissed my class—but not before reminding them what was due Monday morning.

As I was gathering my things, Alex Keaton came to my desk and offered his hand. "Your answer was great copy!"

"I'm sure it was," I said, shaking my head in mild disgust. "I'm sure it was."

I was already regretting my diatribe. I could only hope that, assuming it found its way into print, it was buried on the back pages of the school paper, somewhere between the latest fraternity prank and news of the next faculty hire. Maybe something outrageous would transpire at the upcoming women's lacrosse match that could drown out the ravings of the mad philosophy professor.

- - -

As I left for the library, I wondered if I had just burned a few bridges with my response to the student journalist. Without editorial rights over the story, I had no recourse. My goose was cooked. Then again, I told myself, I wouldn't have had it any other way. I had told the truth.

I found Hap in the stacks.

"Hey," he said as he transferred a book from his cart to the shelf. "What brings you to my neck of woods?"

"Ah," I said, still feeling a little flustered. "I couldn't remember where my Kant class notes were—at home or in the office—so I figured I'd do the next best thing and visit the library."

"I thought you were teaching Socrates right now."

"I am," I said, "but Kant's work complements my Socrates lesson nicely."

"I can see that," Hap replied, emptying the last of the books from the cart. "What constitutes an ethical member of society? To what extent should we follow rules that can hold for everyone? The average person doesn't think about the general laws of nature that guide our experiences. Those laws provide us with a moral blueprint and basis for freedom, immortality, and our relations with a higher being. Heavy stuff. But I suppose it's all part of taking young minds to new heights."

"Exactly," I said, finding myself warming to the topic. "I was going to use Kant's work in tandem with Socrates to add some intellectual meat to my lecture on morality, ethics, and the quest for why people stand up for things, for better or worse. Nothing like adding a few more names to the list to wake up my students and encourage them to consider uncertainty, time, space, and causality. I learned a long time ago that it doesn't matter if they bitch and complain, as long as they keep coming back. All part of stretching them."

Hap led me to the philosophy section and then, leaning slightly, plucked a handful of books from the shelf in front of him. "These should do the trick." He handed me a couple of titles related to Kant and glanced at his watch. "You owe me lunch, right?"

I laughed. "Yeah."

"Well, what are we waiting for?"

We left the library and crossed the quad on our way to the student union building. After I paid for a couple of Cokes at the counter, we spotted a free table next to a long row of windows on the far side of the café and moved to claim it.

Hap draped his overcoat over the chair next to him

and then eyed the stack of books I'd just dropped on our table. "So . . . Immanuel Kant. What does Mr. Kant have to say about your journey with Socrates?"

"Whew!" I said. "I thought you were going to ask a more subjective question regarding your prized shovel, currently hard at work in my backyard. I think to become wise, you have to walk with the wise, not borrow their garden tools unsolicited."

Hap chuckled.

"As you already know by now," I continued, "we can't place limits on philosophy. It's like that in my lectures, research, and writings. That's the beauty of teaching philosophy: It's a constant pursuit of truth and wisdom, not necessarily in that order. No shovel required."

Hap smacked his lips and took a sip of his Coke. "It's all good, brother. Just looking out for you, that's all. So, tell me, how is my favorite nine a.m. class coming along? Are they still spitting nails over copy gate?"

"Surprisingly, good. I'm hard at work with some readings over three distinct periods and trying to get them to relate those to Socrates's quest for ethics and morality in ancient Athens. Next week, I'll bombard them with current events and how they relate to their notion of the status quo. If memory serves me, some nosey research librarian left me a detailed note on the use of current events in my class. Sound familiar? Any more suggestions for me while I'm at it?"

Hap thought for a moment. "Well, let's see. There's Reagan's response to homelessness, the AIDS epidemic, and his indifference toward apartheid in South Africa. Then there's California's ballot initiatives, Prop 187 and Prop 209, which deny education and health benefits to undocumented workers and end affirmative action, respectively. Does that whet your appetite? Seems to me like we have a conservative counterrevolution in the works in America. Better known as a rebuke of the liberalism of the 1960s and early 1970s."

I nodded in agreement. "It looks like the conservatives are all in to reverse the gains made by the civil rights movement and the feminist movement. As the adage goes, everything has a time and place. Revolutions run in cycles, not to mention have ebbs and flows." I thought about my upcoming lectures. "I'll have to do some prepping to balance out the list of current events and have counterarguments ready."

After a long pause, Hap changed the subject. "About that shovel. Have you buried the past in your backyard?"

I smiled to myself. "I'm doing okay. Slowly but surely, I feel like I'm heading in the right direction. The letter from Sarah helped fill in the gaps of the past and settle, once and for all, why she disappeared and cut off all contact. I learned what happened to her and how it worked out."

"Do you have a sense of closure now?"

"I guess so. Her letter reinforced my last conversation with her and how it turned into a referendum on the next step for the FSM and the New Left movement we were building. Unfortunately, I saw my relationship with Sarah as more important than politics and didn't like how extreme the movement was becoming. Sarah, on the other hand, wanted to see the FSM morph into more social justice causes off campus. She wanted to organize opposition to the Vietnam War and build the New Left, including a feminist agenda. Our disagreement over how the left should proceed drove us apart.

"At least, intellectually, I rebuked any overtures to nationalize the FSM. I told her that my involvement was being turned into a circus. People wanted more of me, on and off campus. They wanted me to travel all over the US, visit other campuses, and give speeches and interviews with the press. They wanted me to sit down with university administrators and conduct focus groups. I didn't want that much attention or involvement. I gladly got involved in local protests, marches, debates, and demonstrations at Baker and surrounding communities. Seeking justice on behalf of students' right to free speech, canvassing civil rights funds and support, and calling out the Baker administration for turning the university into a dehumanizing and robotic factory was what I had signed up for and was willing to pursue. But the escalating violence on other campuses and the all-or-nothing mantra turned me off."

Hap appeared to be listening intently but said nothing. Perhaps he was thinking about his own experiences as a student all those years ago.

After a lull in our talk, I ordered us food and, after digging into my turkey sandwich, took a long swig of my Coke. I gazed at Hap, who still looked lost in his thoughts. "Tell me more about your days at Simpson in the 1960s."

He rubbed his chin and sat back in his chair. "Fair is fair. My days in Mississippi taught me to stay in my place. Jim Crow did a number on me and quashed any inclinations I had to take on the authorities. When I turned heads playing football in high school, it took staying in your place to a new dimension. My whole hometown, White and Black alike, was behind me as long as I was scoring touchdowns, running the other team ragged, and helping our team win. To my way of thinking, all I wanted to do was have fun and get good grades in school. Sadly, no one ever asked about my schoolwork or grades. Everyone's attention was on football in the fall and track in the spring."

He paused to gaze out at the quad, which was humming with students. "My football coach was a good guy. In fact, Coach asked me once what I really wanted out of football. I told him that going to college was like going into outer space, since no one in my family had gone or even thought of going. My mother was the only one in the family who supported me."

Hap was smiling, but I spotted what looked like a tear in his eye.

"She told me, 'Carry the football in one hand and books in the other.' When the press clippings started to garner the attention of college scouts, things got interesting. It was the 1960s. Typically no schools in the South actively recruited Black athletes to play football or attend their schools. It was the Midwestern schools and schools out East that recruited me. My coach kept a scrapbook on me and circulated press clippings with some of his former teammates who had gone on to become college assistant coaches. He knew I wanted academics, not football, to lead the way. With that in mind, he used his contacts to get me into Simpson College. He exchanged a few phone calls and game films with his contact there, and it was all set up. I would go to Simpson in the fall of 1965 on a football scholarship. The first two years were good for me. I got good grades, settled on a major, and made second string."

"That's remarkable," I said. "That was right about the time you got injured in Chicago, right?"

"Yeah. The summer of 1967 ruined things for me. But Coach had my back and honored his word on academics coming first and football second. He worked out a deal with the athletic office to have me work part time during the fall and spring semesters and full time in the summers to keep my scholarship intact. I worked as a scout in the press box during football season, I worked the scorer table during basketball season, and I helped the track coach in the equipment room in the spring. I think I told you during our drive to the airport that my mother left Mississippi in the fall of 1968 and joined me at Simpson. We rented an apartment off campus during my senior year."

"After your injury," I said, "did you get involved in student politics or protest?"

"Well, I took a pass. I was told I would do three things when I arrived at Simpson: keep my grades up, avoid getting mixed up in campus politics and partying, and stay healthy so I could keep playing good football. Coach was a big advocate of the college experience. He expected me to grow on every level. It wasn't lost on him that the sixties were a time of trial and tribulation regarding civil rights, Vietnam, and all that. But he told me becoming politically active would come at a cost, especially when it came to athletic scholarships." He shrugged. "I was to lay low, to be seen and not heard."

"Your coach sounds like a decent guy," I added. "A bit of a role model for you, no doubt."

Hap nodded. "His father was a preacher and encouraged him to be intellectual first and athletic second. Being well-read and well-spoken carried a lot of weight with him. He could certainly identify with being poor, having to work hard, and keeping your nose to the grindstone. Coach told me about his college days and how, just like with me, academics meant a lot to him. He told me if I wanted to be active in civil rights, Vietnam, or whatever, I should do it one conversation at a time. In other words, my form of protest was an intellectual one and not one of confrontation."

I smiled. I could relate to Hap's coach and for a moment wished he was seated beside us and partaking in our conversation. Hap, for his part, seemed a little down, like dredging up the past had left him feeling disappointed or wistful somehow. We finished our sandwiches in silence.

Just when I thought the conversation had run its course, a sparkle returned to Hap's eyes. "Coach really encouraged me to read up on the Black activists, like Dr. King, Malcolm X, Stokely Carmichael, and others who were campaigning for social and economic justice. He gave me a list of books to read on all kinds of Black and White authors who were mainstays in campaigns for justice in America. By the time I graduated, I was worried like everyone else about Vietnam. I figured I'd get drafted as soon as college was over, but my injured knee proved to be a blessing in disguise. I was classified as 4F. Plus I was my mother's sole caretaker. Coach wrote a long letter stating my case to the draft board just in case. But all I needed was my doctor's note."

"How did you feel about the war?" I asked.

He frowned, staring down at his empty Coke. "I had mixed emotions about it. I had several friends back in Mississippi that went and came back in a coffin. The ones who came home alive were in bad shape. They ended up hooked on drugs, got into all sorts of mischief, and couldn't find employment. Lots of people turned on the vets coming back from the war, as you know. Too much serious and negative stuff was on TV and in the press. I wanted no part in any of it."

We spoke very little as we walked back to Hickok Hall and the campus library. We were talked out. I felt like I'd been sitting on a psychiatrist's couch and had just undergone an hour's worth of psychoanalysis.

"Take care of my shovel," Hap said as we reached the library. "And call if you need anything."

I gave him a closed-lipped smile. "I will."

Little did Hap know, I had already used the shovel he had loaned me. I planned to return it to him when I could turn the tables and encourage him to bury something that needed to be put to rest. That was what good friends were for: helping when called.

Walking back to my office and then to my car, heading home, I could only wonder what would be waiting for me: a glass of wine, a happy-go-lucky dog, an answering machine full of "dead end" messages?

13

THE OTHER PHONE CALL

"Life contains but two tragedies. One is not to get your heart's desire; the other is to get it."
—Socrates

After teaching my last class of the day and then dropping by my office to gather my things, I took my usual long stroll to the parking lot on the far side of the campus. Parking so far from my office maximized whatever exercise I got each day. Like clockwork, I saw the usual suspects either coming or going from the library, administration building, or Bancroft and Hickok Halls.

Of course, I couldn't resist the opportunity to advance the noble cause of the university by extending a greeting to a former student when I spotted her walking in the opposite direction. "Good afternoon, Ms. Clark."

Jennifer Clark was in her early to mid-twenties—older than most of her fellow undergrads. She wore her dark hair short and typically dressed in dark or muted hues. Today was no different. Her charcoal-gray pea coat hung open, exposing a black turtleneck, short black plaid skirt, and black tights. Her stylish pair of black Doc Martens almost looked like combat boots. In another setting, she might have been a hip, disaffected model charging down the runway.

She paused to size me up. "Hello, Professor Dolan."

I breathed a sigh of relief. At least she had refrained from calling me by my first name. She had a way of treating everyone on campus like they were there to do her bidding. She had aced three of my classes, the last one on existentialism, and seemed to think we were colleagues now.

"Taking anything interesting this semester?" I asked.

She frowned. "Not really. I miss jousting with you in philosophy class."

Jousting? Was that what she called it? Mostly, she had played the role of the tired cynic, and I had tried to steer her back to the core material. "Me too," I lied. "Did you ever follow up on Kierkegaard?"

The best thing she had going for her, in my opinion, was her interest in outside reading—an anomaly among the student body. One day after class she had dropped by my office to ask for a supplemental reading list, and I had eagerly recommended Kierkegaard's classic, *The Sickness Unto Death*.

"I did," she said with a nod. "The only thing worse than death is despair."

I was impressed. "A perfect summary."

"Maybe I should write elevator pitches for a publishing house."

"I've no doubt you could succeed in whatever endeavor you choose."

She shrugged, as if I'd simply spoken the obvious truth, and then squinted at the brightening sky. "Well, I better get going. Nice talking with you, Patrick."

And there it was. A little jab, and she was on her way.

I chuckled to myself. As tiresome as she was, Jennifer was among my students, present and former, which was the only excuse I needed to engage her. I enjoyed bringing a smile, even a smug one, to a young student's face. Sometimes all I needed to accomplish that was to acknowledge their existence or remember their name. Sadly, large universities and colleges tended to evolve into impersonal institutions where people felt like numbers, or worse yet, their presence was taken for granted.

I continued on my way, admiring as I did the rolling hills and trees that surrounded the campus and Decorah. The college sat in a bowl surrounded by cascading hills and beautiful cypress trees. Fall was always spectacular with its beautiful array of colors. Winters, although cold, weren't too bad at Simpson since the hills and trees blocked the wind from affecting three-quarters of the campus. Only the southern portion of campus was wide open, which meant that southerly gusts could be brutally cold, especially during a frigid stretch of weather. A hardy coat and scarf were required to battle the elements.

After reaching my VW in the faculty parking lot, I unlocked the door and ducked inside. The black-and-tan interior, although faded a bit by years of exposure to the Midwest sun, still elicited in me a boyish sense of wonder. I could not help but think about how this car had been with me for decades. But as far as I was concerned, I might as well have stepped into a time machine. I had come to enjoy the conversations and long looks this car elicited from time to time.

I reached into the glove compartment and, after shuffling through a portable case bulging with old cassette tapes, extracted my favorite album among them: Creedence Clearwater Revival's *Green River*. The cassette in my hand was actually my third copy, but it was beginning to wear a little, especially the beginning of side two. There was nothing like a little CCR to take the edge off while heading home after a long day. I could drive fast and hammer it, belt the tunes, or do both to blow off steam.

The drive home took me through downtown, which was lined with small shops noted for their coffee, books, and fashionable clothing. Once or twice a week, I frequented a mom-and-pop café for breakfast before my 9:00 a.m. class. The owners knew me by name and often kept a designated booth open just for me. In fact, they had hung a piece of artwork commemorating my work at the college: a fresco painting of Greeks in togas. From what I had been able to discern upon my last inspection of the piece, Socrates wasn't present, thank God. I could only take so much of him in a day. My other favorite shop was the used bookstore located right next door. I had the luxury of being a preferred customer with a special shelf behind the counter for editions of new or used books that might interest me.

When I got home, I followed my regular routine. I picked up my mail and fetched the morning paper from the bushes. The paperboy hadn't exactly perfected his curve ball yet. I normally didn't mind him missing the front porch on the fly, with the newspaper making a final slide into the welcome mat—at least not on dry days. But rainy days were another matter altogether. I didn't know which I hated more: reading a soggy paper or people arriving late at a class lecture or staff meeting.

After taking Socrates for a short walk, during which he made sure to relieve himself twice, first on an unsuspecting tree trunk and then on a patch of perfectly manicured grass, I sat down on my favorite brown leather chair beside the answering machine and pushed *play*, glass of merlot in hand. On most days, about a half dozen messages awaited me: solicitations, wrong numbers, requests for donation, and reminders or announcements from my department's secretary. From time to time, especially as the end of the week neared, I might get a call from a colleague or friend checking to see if I had any plans for the weekend. Since it was Monday, I didn't expect much besides the regular messages. Thus it was that a smile spread across my face as I listened to the last message of the day and heard the sound of Norah's voice.

"Hey, Patrick. It's Norah. Just checking in to see if you made it back to Decorah and Simpson okay. I hope your trip home was uneventful."

Her voice, calm and consolatory, sounded lovely in my ears. Quite the contrast, I mused, to her sister's. Sarah was a firebrand—a Type A personality who liked to take the lead. As much as I had been attracted to her personality, it had come with its own baggage and, at times, had caused friction and controversy between us. We argued, and we made up. Argued and made up. Our back-and-forth exchanges had taken their toll on our relationship over time. Too many highs and lows.

I made some dinner and fed Socrates his customary dry and wet dog food casserole. He had his spot at one end of the table, and I had mine at the other. We each preferred to eat in silence and thus avoided a one-way conversation about our day. When I had retreated to the study to open the mail, he joined me and lay at my feet. Like most dogs, he liked being in charge when it came to petting and lounging. I petted him, and he lounged. I had given up long ago trying to convince him to help me grade papers. In his own way, he renounced the siren call of academia. He was more of a take-it-as-it-goes canine. Talk about living the life of Riley. Come to think of it, calling him Socrates had been a misnomer in the first place. I should have named him Tom, Dick, or Harry out of spite.

When I had finished with the mail, I turned my attention to the piece of paper I had used to jot down Norah's Chicago-area phone number. Aside from Max, I hardly knew anyone with the 773 area code. Once again, I found myself smiling. I stared at her number, unsure if I should call. After all, I was still sorting out my feelings. But before I could dismiss it, a sense of urgency hit me, and I suddenly realized how much I wanted to talk to her again. I had really enjoyed her company at the memorial service and at the informal reception afterward. I wanted to hear more about her goings-on and not so much about Sarah's. In a small way, I could feel myself moving on from Sarah's death and to the closure I had sought for so long. Yes, I still had lingering questions, but I wasn't sure I wanted to open another can of worms.

After a second glass of wine and grading quantum physics exams on magnetic fusion, I decided to call her.

It rang three times before she picked up and answered in that soothing voice of hers. She sounded like she was right around the corner and not a thousand miles away. "Patrick, so nice to hear from you. I hope you're doing okay."

"I'm doing quite well, thanks. Getting back to my normal routine has helped." I paused to collect my thoughts. "I wanted to thank you once again for the nice talk we had in the garden, you know, before I left."

"Of course," she responded. "It's no problem. I'll be here if you need me again."

Her voice calmed my soul.

"Just saying hello and letting someone know you were thinking about them is medicine enough when recovering from the death of a loved one or family."

"I agree." I fell silent for a few seconds, making room for her to speak next. I tended to take over a conversation on a phone call, but tonight I wanted to listen intently instead of passively. The line between a simple phone call or discussion and the start of a lecture could blur all too easily for me.

"Tell me about your work at Simpson," she said, as if on cue.

"I teach physics and philosophy."

"Do you enjoy the work?"

"I love it." Before I knew it, I was detailing my daily routine and talking about how much my students meant to me.

"You do important work," she said, "especially when considered in the grand scheme of things."

I was glad she couldn't see me blushing. "What about you? What do you do?"

"I'm a curator at the Art Institute of Chicago on Michigan Avenue. I work on Renaissance and medieval art."

I was intrigued. "What does that entail exactly?"

"Well, I'm the one responsible for receiving and dispatching pieces of art not, just around the country but all over the world."

"Wow," I said. "Pretty heady stuff. How long have you been there?"

"Twenty years. I started working there not long after graduating from Northwestern University. I've always loved art. The job requires me to travel abroad three or four times a year to other museums to visit with other curators—which I also love. I try to use the travel to recharge my batteries. Every trip is an awakening of sorts. I especially love anything related to European or Mediterranean culture: the food, the people, and the everyday activities that go on year-round there."

"I get that," I said. "I lived in Germany for a couple of years."

"Really? Germany?" She sounded stunned. "I took you for an Anglophile or Francophile with all the philosophy stuff."

I chuckled. "Philosophy does travel from country to country, namely England, France, Germany, and, of course, Greece. But it was physics that took me to Germany. After my falling out with Sarah and the discontentment I felt with the Free Speech Movement and the direction of the New Left, I decided to enroll in a one-year study abroad program. Since I had taken four years of German in high school, I figured complete immersion would take my mind off of protests and unrest at home. I wanted to forget about Baker. It was too much, and my adviser suggested I leave for a bit."

"That sounds exciting."

"It was. When I got to Germany, I settled in at the Technical University of Munich. I was to study physics as a major and philosophy as a minor. Although I wanted to major in both, my limited German hampered me. It was easier to translate German to survive exams in physics than it was in philosophy. It simply took me too long to read long passages in German each night and take notes, especially ones that were over eighty to a hundred pages. I chose the lesser of two evils, which was physics. Of course, my father was delighted with that."

Norah laughed, and the sound of her voice, so intimate in my ear, left me smiling once again.

I continued with my story. "My studies had me in Europe for three years after I completed my undergraduate studies—the by-product of me staying in Europe over consecutive summers. Thanks to that arrangement, I could take extra courses in advanced math and physics to earn a bachelor's degree and a master's degree at the same time. While I was there, I met my former wife. She was also studying physics and taking advanced courses."

"Oh, I see. What was her name, if you don't mind me asking?"

"Ingrid."

"Ingrid. A classic German and Scandinavian name. What was she like?"

I paused before answering, thinking how strange it was that I'd begun the conversation thinking about Sarah, and now here we were talking about my ex-wife. "She was quiet, intellectual, and very unassuming. Her passion and wide-eyed curiosity in the study of physics attracted me, but I also found her blond hair and deep blue eyes very appealing. My kitchen German was good enough to get a first date, and over time, she helped me perfect my academic German."

"So," Norah said, sounding genuinely curious, "what happened to your marriage? You're obviously no longer with her."

I wasn't sure how to respond. "Well," I said, searching for a way to frame the issue, "like most couples who end up divorced, we didn't have just one problem. Our marriage started out fine, but things became strained not long after we both graduated. I took an academic internship in New York at Columbia

University, where I worked with one of the leading professors in physics. The plan was to collaborate with him for a year before applying to their PhD program. The internship didn't pay well, but at least I got some real job experience. Ingrid was initially pleased to go to the United States. She loved New York City, but then, over time, things started to sour. She couldn't get a job because the visa program was backlogged. With my university pay being what it was, all we could afford was a dump of an apartment near campus."

"A dump?"

"To put it mildly. Our roommates included roaches, mice, and other nasty creatures, and Ingrid was a stickler for maintaining a clean domicile. She cleaned the place until it was spotless, but nothing worked. All it did was make the place tidier for the pests. To make matters worse, our neighbors didn't take kindly to her being German. Far too many were holdovers from World War Two and had long memories. We tried to make the most of it, but I put in too many hours at the university, and she was stuck at home. Compounding things, she was homesick for her family."

I glanced down at Socrates, who was snoring

loudly at my feet, his unruly beard fluttering with each laborious exhale.

Fortunately, Norah couldn't hear him on the other end of the line and continued to ask pertinent questions. "Was there something that finally pushed her over the edge?"

"Yeah, although it was a family matter beyond our control. Her mother was sick, and Ingrid had been the only one to take care of her since Ingrid's father had passed away five years earlier. Her mother sent her letter after letter asking her to return. Finally, Ingrid asked to leave for the summer while I worked several part-time jobs. The idea was for her to look after her mother until she could find another relative to take over. I agreed. I had to. It was the right thing to do. At first, she sent me a letter every week. She called sometimes, too, but international rates were so expensive she could only call sporadically. After a while, the letters stopped. I would call, and her mother would answer. She would tell me Ingrid was out or was at work. I was surprised about the part-time job. When had she gone out and found a job? I found out her mother's only source of income was her deceased husband's military pension. They needed Ingrid's additional income to make ends meet. Before hanging up, I would politely thank her and ask that she call when time permitted.

"Then, one day, I received a thick envelope in the mail with all kinds of official markings on it. Inside were divorce papers. I thought about going back to Germany to see her and try to fix things, but I realized there was nothing to fix. She didn't like living in a dirty apartment building with neighbors who didn't take kindly to foreigners, especially German ones. The civil thing to do was sign them and move on."

"Did you consider moving back to Germany?"

"No," I said, not bothering to soften my response. "That would have been a step backward in my pursuit of the ivory tower. It wasn't that I didn't want to fight to save my marriage. I just didn't think the fight was in *her*. Ultimately, I chose the path of least resistance and let the divorce play itself out."

Norah was silent for a moment. "Sounds like the women in your life have a habit of walking off and leaving you high and dry."

I shook my head in disbelief, shocked by the comment, but soon I couldn't stop laughing. She had nailed the problem. The two most important women in my life—Sarah and Ingrid—had each in turn left me. It was a painful truth, but something about Norah's delivery eased the pain. It was like she was saying, "Shit happens, and now it's time to move on." She wasn't talking *at* me; she was talking *with* me—and helping me laugh at myself and my past. Not too many people could do that, and I found myself taken by it.

The moments seemed to fly by with Norah, and by the time our conversation had run its course, I glanced down at my watch and was surprised to note that we had been speaking for two hours.

"Thanks again for reaching out, Norah," I said. "Talking with you has worked wonders for my spirits. I hope the same was true for you."

"It was a pleasure, Patrick. Let's talk again soon."

As I hung up the phone, I felt lighter on my feet. I couldn't remember the last time I had connected so well and so easily with someone, and my mouth seemed stuck in a perma-grin. Two hours had felt like two minutes. As I put the telephone receiver down, I could not help but to think about how life was indeed good. I looked down at Socrates, who had awakened from his nap. He looked back at me. He wagged his tail and to my amazement, cocked his head and rendered what I thought was a shit-eating grin. It was like he was acknowledging me for moving on.

14

9:00 A.M. PHILOSOPHY #3

"Envy is the ulcer of the soul."
—Socrates

There came a moment in every class when I would find out just how much homework my students had finished. As I surveyed my philosophy class the next morning, I wondered how deeply they had immersed themselves in their studies. Would I be impressed by their thorough explanations, or would I hear crickets in response to my questions? There was nothing like listening to the sound of my own voice because no one had come to class prepared. Often, I relied on written cues—short phrases or one-word titles—to test their knowledge and their confidence in that knowledge. And today was no exception. On the blackboard behind me I had written the following names:

Bruni

Monette

Marila

Hegel

Voltaire

Nietzsche

But this morning I wanted to do more than tease free little factoids and strains of thought. I wanted to have a conversation.

The students stared back at me with a mixture of disinterest and trepidation. Some, dressed in sweats or nursing a Styrofoam cup of coffee, looked like they had just crawled out of bed. They were groggy and bleary-eyed and seemed to wither under the bright overhead lights. Others, pen in hand and eyes fixed forward, looked better prepared. Perhaps this was their second class of the day, and they had already established a morning groove.

I trained my eyes on Denise Tate, my formerly reserved freshman no longer trying to disappear in the back row and decided to start with her. I had learned by now that I could put her on the spot without overwhelming her. "So, Denise, the last time we met, you told us briefly, with Roger's help, about Socrates's origins and his plight with the Athenian authorities. Excellent job, both of you. Now, looking at the board, does anybody want to start off with what you read and how it applies to Socrates?"

"I'll go first," offered Ronny Jefferson, dressed as usual in his letterman's jacket.

Previous experience suggested that Ronny might know only a minimum of the material, and he wanted to establish what he did know right now, so he could recede from the discussion as it grew more nuanced. But I didn't mind. I appreciated anybody who was willing to get the proverbial ball rolling.

"Okay, Ronny, what do you have?"

"Bruni. According to what I read, he was a Renaissance scholar who helped rediscover Plato's work, which discusses his studies under Socrates. It was in Plato's *Phaedo*, *Republic*, and *Symposium*. They were drawn into Socrates's teachings that emphasize two major principles." He paused to stare down at his notepad, upon which I could see barely legible handwritten notes. "'There is no greater evil one can suffer than to hate reasonable discourse,' and 'With wisdom we have real courage and moderation and justice—in a word, true virtue.'"

I raised an eyebrow, impressed. Maybe he had done more than a cursory reading. I decided to press Ronny further. "And what virtues would they be, according to Socrates?"

Ronny squinted up at the ceiling like someone foraging in his mind for the faintest recollection. Then his eyes widened with relief that he had found what he was looking for. "Courage, temperance, prudence, justice, and wisdom." The words came tumbling out like he was worried he'd forget them if he didn't recite them quickly enough.

Denises's hand shot up. "Don't forget that Socrates argued about what leads to these virtues. We must be knowledgeable."

"Explain," I said.

She nodded, clearly just getting started. "We need to recognize when we are ignorant and need to change our state of being from being ignorant, either intellectually or spiritually."

At least two students had done the reading.

I offered a cautious smile. "Okay, so far, I like what I'm hearing. Let's look at what Socrates inferred with the notion of spirituality or, better yet, the notion of gods or god. Anyone got any ideas on that subject based on the readings?"

"I do, Professor," Thomas Brooks said after raising his hand. From what I could tell, Thomas was one of the more gifted students in class, but he wasn't one to showcase his knowledge. He picked his moments, and now appeared to be one of them. "According to the French satirist Voltaire, Socrates was a theist who believed in a deity that intervened in creation. In fact, Voltaire wrote a satirical three-act play called *Socrates* to give what he thought was an account of Socrates and his plight. Voltaire argued that Socrates was monotheistic and that his trial was more a religious persecution than a political one. His play was heavy with his contempt for government authority and organized religion. Looking at his work, you could argue that he viewed Socrates as a moral individual brought up on bogus charges by corrupt and immoral leaders who didn't want anyone to question the status quo of Athens or Greek life."

"Good account of Voltaire, Thomas." I motioned to the blackboard. "Let's return to our list. Who isn't accounted for so far?"

Another hand shot up. It belonged to Mary Higgins, a bookish young woman with wire-framed glasses that made her dark-brown eyes look tiny. She made a habit of ending most of her sentences on an up note, as though she were asking a question. "Hegel?"

"Okay," I said, turning toward her. "So, let's have it. What did Hegel have to say about our dear friend Socrates?"

Mary straightened at her desk. "Well, for one, he credited Socrates with introducing the principle of free subjectivity?"

"What, according to Hegel, is free subjectivity?" I asked.

"Yeah, it's our idea of self-determination? Self-determination is the freedom an individual has to determine the conditions of their own life. Of course, to do this, you have to declare your ignorance and show a willingness to find virtues worth pursuing through acquiring wisdom? But he found one major obstacle? According to Hegel, an individual who pursues this path could be, or would be, considered an enemy of the state since his or her efforts obstruct the way of life shaped by institutions and laws of the state? Freedom and the pursuit of virtues associated with them aren't relative to the individual; they're relative to what the state has to say and the institutions that support it, back it up, and, more importantly, tell us what is important and not important?"

I managed to ignore Mary's peculiar style of speaking, where her tone presented everything as if they were questions, and focus on her statements. "Excellent rendition on the work of Hegel and its application to Socrates. Anybody want to add to it or apply it to other readings?"

Mark Birch joined the discussion. "Professor, what about Nietzsche and his resentment of Socrates and his critique of his influence on Western culture?"

I smiled. "Mark, the floor is all yours."

"From the readings, I understand that Nietzsche held Socrates in contempt for what he did to Greek civilization during the fifth and fourth centuries BC and after. He argued that Socrates turned the discipline of philosophy on its ear by using rationalism and intellectualism instead of naturalism to explain the measure of human existence, its lack of reason, and its suffering."

"Sounds like you looked into *The Birth of Tragedy* and *The Twilight of the Idols*."

"Yeah," Mark said with a shrug. "But I didn't read all of them. That would have taken forever."

A few of his classmates giggled at the remark.

"Perfectly understandable. What did you learn?"

"Well," Mark began, "when you think about it, Nietzsche wasn't a huge fan of Socrates, and he rebuffed Socrates's connection of reason to virtue and the pursuit and acquisition of happiness in your life."

I searched the attentive faces in the classroom, took a pause, and noted all the pens flying across the page as Mark finished. I was thrilled by the students' answers so far and how much effort they were putting into the material.

I went to the board and wrote down the following:

reason + virtue = happiness

I then proceeded to announce the next assignment. "Class," I said, "I want you to look at your own existence here at Simpson and apply what you've learned to date and return to class with your own thoughts on Socrates's application of ignorance, the pursuit of wisdom, and the acquisition of virtues."

After being dismissed, the students packed up their books and filed out the door. Surprisingly, I didn't hear any grumbling or complaints. As they left, I paused to take stock of what I had heard. I shook my head in wonder, impressed by the responses to my queries, and smiled as I gathered my coat and briefcase. I couldn't help but wonder what Socrates would have thought about the day's lesson. All told, I was pretty sure he would have been proud—although perhaps not as proud as I was.

15

HERE WE GO AGAIN!

"The greatest way to live with honor in this world is to be what we pretend to be."
—Socrates

On Thursday morning before class, I was summoned to the dean's office before 9:00 a.m. His secretary instructed me over the phone to arrive at 8:30 sharp. I knocked on the door at 8:25, determined not to be late.

The door opened a moment later, and there stood the dean, a slight man with a crooked spine and thinning gray hair.

"Good morning, Dean Russell," I said.

"Hello," he replied in a low-key voice.

We shook hands, and after he retreated to his oversized mahogany desk, which matched the bookshelves behind him, I sat down in the spindly folding chair across from him. The wooden expanse between us was largely bare, with only a couple of family photos and a file folder cluttering his desk.

I held my breath. Being summoned by the dean of the department in the middle of the semester was almost never a good thing.

"I've got a busy day planned," he began in a reedy tone, "so let's get to it." He opened the file folder in front of him. "Do you know what this is?" he asked, pointing with his eyes at the document inside the folder.

"I haven't the foggiest."

"It's a campus police report that my office received yesterday afternoon. Would you like me to summarize it for you?"

I didn't like the game he was playing but had no choice but to play along. "By all means."

"It seems campus police had to write a summons for over thirty students who were disturbing the peace in the student union building. Apparently, they were protesting the campus administration and demanded to have a list of their grievances heard immediately. The dean of students was summoned to the student union in order to quell the protest and restore order. The protesting students had prepared a list of grievances supported by over one hundred signatures. The arresting officer notes in the report here that the line to sign their manifesto was over five hundred students long. In response, campus police stopped the signature signing because they were afraid more students would join in. They weren't equipped to manage a disturbance of that magnitude."

I felt my mouth drop in astonishment. I was speechless.

"The attending officer wrote that he was relieved there wasn't an all-out food fight, because he would have had to arrest them all and take them to the student detention center and place them in holding tanks." Dean Russell paused to look up from the report. "How the hell do you put over a hundred co-eds in lockup, for Christ's sake?" He waved his right hand in the air, as if dismissing the question, and then continued. "It also states here that when the students were being written up, several of them credited you with awakening them to the rigors of using academics to enlighten and inspire their understanding of their plight on campus. Another entry states here that the students were chanting, 'Socrates, Socrates, Socrates!' When the attending officer asked who Socrates was, one of the students said he would have to take your class to find out."

I opened my mouth to speak, still struggling to find the words, but he cut me off.

"There's more. Several of these so-called Socrates *proteges* managed to appropriate some tablecloths and fashion them into togas. They then jumped onto a student union dinner table and chanted, 'Down with the man! Up with Socrates!' The arresting officer states that he laughed so hard that he didn't have it in him to do anything about it. It states here that he elected to let this one slide due to student stupidity of the highest order, with or without academic guidance." He slid the report toward me to give me a closer look at a handful of mug shots, a few of which I recognized as belonging to my students. The report dubbed them the Fab Five.

I sank in my chair. I usually only saw Dean Russell once or twice a semester. The fact that he hadn't hired me—and that I had no PhD and was retained year to year—made things rather interesting, to say the least.

I took a deep breath and tried to fashion a plausible response. "I've been lecturing on Socrates and his efforts to acquire virtue and challenge Athenian authorities on the value of education, morality, and ethics. It sounds like some of my students took it to heart and got carried away."

The dean frowned, clearly unconvinced.

"It appears they turned their homework on the status quo into a manifesto," I continued, still hoping to mollify him. "The petition signing is news to me. I have no idea how my class got involved."

The dean leaned back in his chair and paused for a moment to digest what I had said. "Professor Dolan, you've been here twenty years now. From what I understand, your primary job is teaching physics and remedial mathematics, with one or two classes in philosophy each semester. You don't have tenure, and from what I can tell, you're considered a legacy hire by the former Simpson College president, who knew you from your graduate studies at Columbia. It seems you physics and math guys stick together through thick and thin." He closed the folder in front of him. "I have it on good authority that you were quite infamous as a radicalized undergraduate at Baker University back in the day."

Here we go, I thought to myself.

"You've managed to keep your personal history under wraps, from the sounds of it. I assume you'd rather not have it known among the faculty or students. Am I correct?"

I rushed to agree with him. "Yes, sir, you're most correct. It's something that I would rather remain buried in the past."

"Professor Dolan, I'm fine with the past remaining in the past. That being said, I'm going to have to write up this whole matter in my daily report to the university provost's office. It's my hope that whoever is behind this student protest has quieted down and that this is the end of it. If not, you're going to have to explain yourself and your incendiary lectures to the higher-ups. Since I'm a humanities professor in training and trade, I get what you're trying to accomplish, and I applaud you for trying to get your students to think, read, and write critically—or in this case, use what they're learning and apply it to their own lives. But standing on tables, signing a protest manifesto to the college provost, and resisting arrest all in the name of Socrates isn't what I, the provost, and the college president, I'm sure, had in mind."

I nodded and stood up to leave. My head was spinning. Here I had been admiring my work only a day earlier, and now this debacle.

Just as I turned to leave, the dean asked me one more question. "Why didn't you finish your PhD while you were at Columbia?"

I winced, swallowing hard. "I made it to ABD. I had my preliminary research done when my wife left me. I tried to bury myself in my research and start my dissertation. Then I was hit with another problem: My dissertation proctor took sick leave with cancer and never returned. I searched for a new dissertation chair in the midst of an all-out political war between the department leads, since my work covered both physics and mathematics. My former chair had ties to both disciplines and carried a lot of weight. What was approved beforehand when he was still there was perfectly fine. When he left, there was an interdisciplinary conflict over my thesis. I was told I had to start all over and pick a new topic. As a result, all my research was null and void.

"Between the divorce and unfinished dissertation,

I dropped out, thinking I would return in a year. I got a call from a friend of mine on staff here at Simpson saying they needed someone to run the remedial math program here. I was promised full-time hours as a math lab instructor, with hours as a lecturer in physics, and if the philosophy department needed help, I could pitch in from time to time. I came, I liked it, and I stayed. Too much time had passed to consider going back to finish. I guess you could say I climbed the ivory tower halfway and stopped."

After skulking out of Dean Russell's office, I made a beeline to my 9:00 a.m. class. I walked in and stared at my students.

No one said a word.

I sat down at my desk, paused to savor a long drink of my still-warm coffee, and then opened my satchel to retrieve my lecture notes. The fact that I hadn't started right away let them know that I was more than a little thrown by recent events. I had yet to receive their side of the story.

Finally, I stood to address them. "I would like you all to know that this isn't an inquisition or a trial. I was summoned to my department dean's office this morning regarding a student protest led by my students in the student union building. It's my understanding that yesterday there was, for a lack of a better word, an *insurrection* in the name of Socrates. Based on the blotter report from the campus police, five of you were duly named and charged. I must say, your mug shots on the blotter report look noteworthy. Does anyone of the so-called Fab Five mentioned in the campus police report care to discuss this matter? For those of you who were lucky enough to miss all the fun, you may leave or stay—it's your call. In fact, if you elect to stay, you might learn something or, better yet, help me sort this all out. Who cares to go first?"

To my surprise, Denise Tate raised her hand first. I hadn't figured her to be someone to start an insurrection, but the plucky freshman continued to surprise me.

"Professor, it's not as bad as it seems. As far as the five of us are concerned, we were sitting at a table in the student union working on our current events, status quo, and personal lives portion of your latest assignment. Some students overheard us and asked to join in. We didn't think anything of it and allowed them to sit in. It turns out that one of the students works for the campus newspaper. He whipped out a pad of paper and pen and started to write stuff down. I didn't want to be rude and tell him to put it away. When Thomas asked if he minded putting it away, he argued that other students on campus need to hear about this Socrates stuff. 'Besides,' he said sarcastically, 'your professor isn't exactly teaching a standing-room-only course. From what I hear, philosophy is a dead subject these days.'

"The next thing I knew, one of his friends sat down and started to listen in. He mentioned that he could canvass students in the student union about their issues with the status quo on campus and use the results as survey data. He then walked across the commons and returned with a table and chairs to start canvassing. Another friend of his stood up and started to line up other students in front of the table, asking them to think about their issues and demands regarding the status quo on campus. Before long, over a hundred students were lined up.

"The canvasser was on his third page when all hell broke loose. Student union staff asked students to go back to their seats and take their survey outside. Next thing we knew, someone yelled, 'Socrates rules!' The whole line joined the chant, and before long, most of those in the student union were chanting the same thing. Then the campus police showed up to restore order. Of course, when asked who started it all, everyone pointed at us sitting at the table. We figured we would be let go if we just answered their questions. Sadly, some students got onto tables and started to chant 'Socrates!' again. They had made togas out of tablecloths, which got the student union staff quite upset. Just before the campus police showed up, some students had started a snake dance through the cafeteria, which was over one hundred students long. Before long, more campus police showed up and started to arrest students for disorderly conduct. I don't think things would have been so bad, but someone started to throw food and push back at the arresting officers. The Socrates chant gave way to 'Pigs! Pigs!' As you can imagine, the campus police didn't care for that at all." Denise gave me an imploring look as she finished her summary. "Professor, please trust that we meant no harm, that we took our class assignment and our discussions to heart, and that they were relevant and timely. We had no control over those students who butted in and took things too far."

After a few more students piped up with what they

had seen and heard during and after the protest, I paused to assess what I had heard.

"Class, you can rest assured that your work was greatly appreciated. This incident will, I hope, work itself out." I shook my head, barely able to suppress a grin. "The next time you consider doing a group discussion or project, be wary of who's listening and how they might react to what they hear."

Ryan raised his hand to offer his two cents. "Think of it this way, Professor. No standing on police cars were involved, and no grandiose speeches were offered. It was a bloodless protest."

I resisted the urge to reprimand him for the wisecrack, reminding myself that my students were young kids full of energy, enthusiasm, and conviction. I had entertained similar thoughts and feelings in my youth, after all.

I left Hickok Hall and walked straight to the campus police office to discuss the matter of my five offending students.

The desk sergeant, a portly man with dark hair and a mustache to match, gave me a fair hearing. "I can assure you the Fab Five are safe."

"They won't be punished further?"

He nodded. "They were the most obedient of the bunch and the most cooperative. In fact, they tried to take the blame for the whole incident. That won't happen. We know for a fact that some of the other students that joined the protest are repeat offenders who've been in trouble for previous disturbances on and off campus. Your students will have their summons dropped as a warning and won't be reported to the provost's office."

I felt a surge of relief. "I can't thank you enough, Officer."

As I walked back to my office to collect my things before heading over to the math lab, I was suddenly overcome with a sense of déjà vu. I thought about my talk with Dean Russell. I had a good thing going at Simpson, and I didn't want anything or anyone to ruin it. But my past had once again reared its ugly head.

16

COME SEPTEMBER

"Those who are hardest to love need it the most."
—Socrates

When I got home that afternoon, I took Socrates for a quick walk and then checked the messages on my answering machine. There was only one, and I recognized Hap's baritone voice immediately.

"Socrates! Socrates! Socrates! Comrades, spare the women and children. Take no prisoners! Burn the student union to the ground!" He unleashed a hearty laugh before continuing. "Mind if I drop by later today?

I want to grab my shovel in case you're thinking of digging a hole and burying yourself in it."

I shook my head and laughed. With only three weeks to go, I could only hope the rest of the semester would go more smoothly.

About an hour later, I heard a knock at the front door.

When I opened it, Hap stood on the front porch with a bottle of red wine in his right hand. "I figured you might need a drink to settle your nerves or better yet, drown your sorrows."

We retreated to the back porch to discuss recent events at Simpson and put it all to rest.

"I guess I shouldn't have encouraged you to use current events in class," he said with an apologetic laugh.

I laughed along with him. "It's funny. Over the years, the Socrates assignment has, to a certain degree, gotten stale. More and more undergrads don't take advantage of the status quo portion of the assignment and its relationship to their personal lives. Outside of a few heated moments, when students recount their own connections with one another in class, nothing has ever come to pass." I paused to take a sip of merlot. "So,

Dean Russell summoned me to his office before class this morning."

"I hope my name didn't come up," Hap replied, "and the fact that it was my idea that the students use the assignment and relate it to their own lives."

"It didn't," I said. "Although now that you mention it, I wish I would have deflected some of the blame."

We sat in silence, and I wondered about my motives. Was I using the Socrates assignment to justify my actions in 1964 at Baker? I let the fleeting thought pass, since I didn't want to discuss it any further.

Perhaps sensing my wish to change subjects, Hap did just that. "So," he ventured, "have you heard from Norah lately? If you ask me, she likes you and wants to get to know you better."

"Nah," I said. "She's just a family member of Sarah's looking out for me. She's thinking of the impact of a letter overdue by about twenty-seven years. We did talk on the phone the other day. It was nice." I left it at that. I didn't feel like I could give the matter much thought until I had sorted through the recent events at Simpson.

We talked for a bit longer, and Hap left with his shovel.

I spent the rest of my evening studying, grading papers, and drinking more wine, and as the night wore on, I found myself thinking about Hap's comment about Norah. Maybe he was right. Hap had a way of tapping into things I usually missed.

To put his theory to the test, I took out a pen and wrote Norah a thank-you card for calling and checking up on me. I kept it simple and direct.

The next day, thinking I would either hear back or not, I put the letter in the mail. Then I went about my day, and much to my relief, the rest of the day and that week went by without any further surprises from my students. Before leaving campus Friday afternoon, I decided to call the provost from my office and discuss a long talk I'd had with my students. I was no fan of Beau Chesterman, but I thought it a wise policy to remain ahead of the problem with the powers that be.

"I just wanted to assure you that I won't encourage this type of activity again," I said after reviewing the matter.

"Don't give it a second thought," Chesterman said, surprising me with his generous tone. "In the grand scheme of things, some food was tossed, a few police feathers were ruffled, and some tables were dented.

Besides, Professor Dolan, it could have been worse. It's not like we're living in the sixties or seventies. Now *that* was a dangerous time on college campuses."

I stared in disbelief at the receiver in my hand. As far as I knew, Chesterman had no clue about my involvement in the student protests of my youth. I decided to keep it that way and politely ended the conversation.

After hanging up the phone, I took out the Socrates Manifesto secured by the campus police from one of the so-called Socrates 100. There it was: a smartly written list of their grievances and demands. In no logical order, it read:

- *We want the student union food menu to be changed. It's overpriced, and the portion sizes are too small.*
- *We want the library to be open twenty-four hours a day, seven days a week.*
- *We want better recreation opportunities on campus. The intramurals are stale and need to be revamped.*
- *We want Simpson Dead Week before finals to be started two days earlier. In other words, no*

new material after our last class on Wednesday the week prior.

- *We want more open seats on the Student Senate. This includes allowing commuter students to take part.*
- *We want the administration to send a representative to the Decorah City Council and have them pass an ordinance that locks in rent rates for Simpson students. If a student wishes to renew their lease, the property owner should not be able to raise the rent by more than 5 percent of the original amount.*
- *Finally, we demand that . . .*

The final bullet point had been left unfinished. No doubt the campus police had gained the upper hand, and the list had been apprehended before it could be finished. The list was pretty naïve, I thought. Laughable, even. No mention had been made of securing civil rights on or off campus, no antiwar or anti-imperial sentiments had been shared, and nothing had been said about women's rights.

The concerns of students in the early 1990s, I couldn't help thinking, were relatively trivial. It seemed young Americans had moved on to better things—or at least thought they had. The AIDS epidemic, sales of arms to rogue nations to fight an illegal war on drugs, skyrocketing homelessness in America, the pending crisis in the Middle East—all appeared unimportant to students. But as long as there were humans, I told myself, there would be something to protest. Even in Socrates's time, people had complained about their daily lives.

- - -

Every afternoon for the next three weeks, I eagerly sorted through my mail as soon as I got home from campus. And every afternoon, I found nothing from Norah. No letter. No card. No missive of any kind. Thus, I put the letter-writing campaign to rest, along with the idea of Norah liking me.

The semester ended uneventfully, thank God, and after finals were over and I had finished doling out grades, I spent a few days preparing for my annual trek to New York City to see my parents during winter break. Just before I left, I dropped off grumpy Socrates with a friend, canceled my newspaper subscription, and filled out a form at the post office to hold my mail until I returned.

My trip to New York was mundane but restful. My parents, at an advanced age, considered sitting in their kitchen and listening to me talk about my career and my travails a treasured holiday long overdue. They weren't much for going out anymore. My dad, a diehard Yankees and Giants fan, spent his free time listening to the games on the radio, reading books on Zen, and drinking homemade wine. While I was home, I managed to get him outside for short walks in the brisk evening air. During our walks, I let him do all the talking. He liked to talk about life when I was a kid, current events, or how my mother was trying to get him to quit smoking. Nothing too heavy—just regular father-son stuff.

On the other hand, my mother was a tougher sell when talking about my life, especially my romantic relationships—or the lack thereof. She didn't beat around the bush. "So, Patrick, how is your love life? I don't want you to grow old without someone being there for you."

We were loading the dishwasher after dinner on a cloudy winter evening.

"Mother, stop."

She ignored my request. "I just read an article last

week about people who live alone and don't get out much. It's not healthy. There are all kinds of ills associated with a reclusive lifestyle."

I'd been here countless times before and waited for her to finish before serving up a reply I'd worked out in advance. "Mother, you know I'm busy enough with my teaching career. I have plenty of colleagues and friends I spend time with. If there was someone who came along that was worthy of my time in the love department, you'd be the first to know."

She offered an impatient frown. "You know, Patrick, I've given up waiting on you to have grandkids. I'll take you having someone to spend your golden years with just the same."

I was tempted to tell her about Norah but elected not to. What was there to talk about?

"I still don't understand why you and Ingrid divorced. As far as I'm concerned, people in a committed relationship don't just up and quit on someone when things get thick. You stay and work things out."

I bit my tongue and said nothing.

After finishing with the dishes, I grabbed a book and took up a position beside a window overlooking

Central Park on the East Side. I loved looking out over the park, even in the winter when the red maples were bare. I also enjoyed using New York's subway system, browsing bookstores, and touring museums and cultural sights. Earlier in the day, while visiting a small art gallery, I had found my thoughts returning to Norah. While staring at a painting I normally would have passed by, I had wondered what Norah would think of it. Now, staring out at Central Park in the evening gloom, I was tempted to borrow my parents' phone and call her just to say hello and to see how she was doing. I thought better of it and let it go. I didn't want my parents, especially my mother, to overhear something while I was on the phone.

After a few days in New York, I returned home to Decorah to a snowstorm. Luckily for me, the spring semester at Simpson wouldn't start for another ten days. Socrates ignored me for about a week—punishment for leaving him with a stranger—but eventually we returned to our regular routine. As the snow melted outside, I had plenty to keep me busy: returning phone calls, opening mail, and prepping for my courses.

When Socrates returned to his usual self, he joined

me in the study and assumed his normal position. He sat on my books. He sat on my mail. He pretended to be a lapdog and sat on my lap, demanding I pet him nonstop. Late one evening before bedtime, he kept scratching at something that had fallen behind my desk. It turned out to be a letter from Chicago postmarked while I had been away in New Jersey. It was pink and smelled like lilac. It was from Norah. I opened it immediately.

Dear Patrick,

I wanted to drop you a quick note to say hi and let you know how much I appreciated your kind words. Yes, I also enjoyed our phone conversation and would like to talk again soon. The reason for my delay in getting back to you is related to the museum business. I just returned from a three-week trek to Europe to conduct research on future exhibits and talk shop with other curators.

My trip took me to Greece, France, and England. Being gone was nice but trying to catch up after you return is a drag. Your note put a smile on my face. I'm going to send you a little present I picked up during my travels. I think you'll like it. Be sure to say hi to

Socrates for me and keep your students knee-deep in essays and books trying to figure out the mysteries of physics and philosophy.

Bye for now,
Norah

I put down the letter, feeling pleased. For the first time in years, I felt I had someone special in my life. What exactly that entailed remained to be seen. I wasn't one to get ahead of myself, even when my heartstrings had been plucked.

True to her word, Norah sent a parcel, which arrived a few days later. I opened the box immediately, eager to know what treasure lay inside. After rooting through gobs of packing material, I found it.

"No shit!"

To my amazement, it was a bust of Socrates, and it had come straight from Greece.

Attached to the bust was a note from Norah:

Patrick, in case you forgot what Socrates looked like back in the day. If you don't mind me saying so, he was quite homely. At least his words and arguments were more noteworthy.

Talk soon,
Norah

I placed the bust on my desk in the study. To show his displeasure at the ugly new decor, Socrates growled at the bust. He continued to paw at it until I put a sack over it. I couldn't wait to take it to my office on campus for all to see. In the meantime, I decided to call Norah and thank her for the kind gesture.

Once again, she answered on the third ring.

"Norah," I said, "I wanted to call and let you know how much I appreciated you thinking of me. The bust of Socrates is awesome! I plan to display it proudly."

"I thought you'd like it," she replied with a giggle. "I don't visit museum gift shops per se. I bought the Socrates bust in a little gift shop near the Parthenon from a kind old man who assured me that he had made it by hand. In fact, he took me to the back of his shop to show me his bust molds. He demonstrated to me how he made his busts from molds, plaster . . . well, using various materials. I assured him with my art history training, I was well-versed in painting, sculpture, and drawing. This Greek gentleman was so kind, he even had me sit down at his potter's wheel so I could get my hands wet in clay. He wanted me to remember how the clay feels in your fingers and hands. I really enjoyed that."

I could hear the smile in her voice.

"Apart from that, the trip was fine, and I'm glad to be back home."

I laughed out of pure pleasure.

"What's so funny?"

"I enjoy listening to your voice," I answered. "It's nice to hear someone so excited about their work. It's refreshing."

"Thanks," she said, sounding pleased and surprised by my reaction. "I'm infamous for talking too much about my work. Sometimes I don't know when to shut up!" She laughed.

"No worries. Keep talking. I'd love to hear all about your travels to Europe and beyond. I haven't been out of the country since I returned from Germany years ago. I'm due to travel again soon—long overdue. Got any ideas?"

Norah paused to think. "Well, you should think about what you teach and pick places that might help illustrate what you talk about. In my opinion, we sometimes get so rooted in what we do—in your case, teach—that we forget to go to the world beyond the book or what we know. There's a saying: 'You do your best thinking when the rubber hits the road.' I've found that I always come back refreshed from my trips. They remind me why I love art history and the artwork at the Art Institute in Chicago."

"Advice well taken, Norah, especially from you."

"Hah!" She sounded quite pleased with herself.

"Well, I don't mean to cut you short, Norah, but I need to grade some papers. Can I call you back this weekend so we can talk more?"

"Sure."

I couldn't tell if she sounded eager or not.

"Sundays work best for me," she added. "I usually go to the Art Institute on Saturdays to get some work done when the office is closed."

"All right then. Sunday it is. Take care and stay safe."

Our conversation continued over the phone and in letters, and we spent the first few weeks of spring semester talking about our daily adventures and sharing our passion for work.

During one of our phone calls, Norah asked me

what I was doing for spring break. "You should come to Chicago and see what it has to offer," she suggested.

I agreed, and we made plans to see each other in the middle of March.

That spring break, while my students had fun at the beach with drinks, dancing, and God knows what, I spent three days visiting museums, boating on the Chicago River, and dining at local hole-in-the-wall restaurants. I thoroughly enjoyed myself. The wonderful part was being in Norah's company, and I could tell that the pleasure wasn't all mine.

We talked and talked, and what struck me was just how deep the talks became. They flowed so naturally, each of us listening to and talking with the other intently and patiently. On a few occasions, I grabbed her hand and held it while we talked or while we strolled the sidewalks. It wasn't long before I had my arm around her shoulder. We were becoming friendlier and getting closer with each passing day.

While in Chicago, I also got a chance to visit Norah's family. It was nice to visit without the cloud of a funeral hanging over us. I met with aunts and uncles, along with her sister Hannah, for an extended period of time. We shared family meals and visited the garden at Norah's house. They treated me well and seemed pleased that Norah had invited me back to Chicago. But, on more than one occasion, I could see the aunts huddled together and exchanging smirks. Given the looks on their faces and the whispering that went with them, it was clear they were talking about me and my time spent with Norah.

When I returned to Decorah, I once again had to prepare for my classes on Monday when I would have rather been doing something else. But instead of becoming stressed about it, I devoted my thoughts to Norah and my visit to Chicago.

Norah was so different from Sarah. Not necessarily in a bad way. Simply different. I couldn't get over how, in such little time, I had come to know her. Yet it felt as though I had known her for years. We were each professional, unmarried, and in love with our work. At forty-seven, I was seven years older than her. It was nice to have someone and something to look forward to each night, whether that meant reading one of her letters or talking with her on the phone.

Once Hap heard about the growing relationship between us, he felt compelled to offer his advice. I was picking up a book at the library one day in May after the semester ended when he took me aside. "You should invite her to Decorah for a long weekend this September," he suggested. "Take her to a football game. Hell, you have faculty tickets on the fifty-yard line. Besides, you know how to tailgate and throw a good house party." He grinned.

Why hadn't I thought of that? He was right. I would ask her down for a visit. I looked at the calendar and saw our homecoming game was scheduled for the end of September against our archrival, Cornell. I made a note on my desk calendar to call the athletic office first thing Monday and arrange for tickets.

I couldn't help but sense that something was happening between Norah and me. We weren't just trading phone calls and swapping stories about work and our lives; we were checking up on each another more frequently and making plans to see more of each other. The wonderful thing about being older was that I had been around the block a few times and was able to cut to the chase. When it came to chemistry with another person, you either had it or you didn't. I planned to take it slow with Norah and appreciate what I had. I would think big, as the saying went, and act small.

17

"TOWNIES"

"To be is to do."
—Socrates

I had to admit I wasn't the most sociable man in town at times. My life off campus was most comfortable when I was seen and not heard. But that wasn't always possible. While I liked visiting the local café and bookstore on occasion, I chose to limit my interaction with the townsfolk. I did take time to say hello to people, namely students who knew me or of me, along with those I'd shared a meal with, purchased a book from, or been served by. It could be challenging to start up a conversation that involved my college work. The subjects of physics and philosophy weren't exactly easy conversation starters for most people.

Not surprisingly, I'd found that the Decorah locals had mixed feelings about Simpson College and its students. They loved the business the college brought in the form of tax revenue, cheap labor, and tourists, but that was about it. At the end of the day, they tolerated the students, as long as they pursued their academic affairs on campus and kept their youthful mischief within the confines of Simpson's hallowed halls.

My being seen and not heard was sorely put to the test after spring break. Several of my students asked me to speak on their behalf to some of the local businesses that had banned them from visiting their stores for disturbing the peace. I found out that some of my students had gotten into a heated conversation with one of the owners of the bookstore and an eavesdropping café patron. Their ill-fated discussion centered on hourly wages, due process, and freedom of speech. As you can imagine, the young minds eager to debate controversial subjects with the older crowd soon got out of hand. After the owner threw out the students, he contacted a few of his business associates and had them blacklisted.

To make matters worse, the owner's friend was the brother-in-law of one of the campus police officers who had arrested one of my students. Soon enough, the talk of the Decorah townies was how some of my students had staged an insurrection on campus and had taken it to downtown Decorah. To add insult to injury, I was again named the inspiration of this so-called insurrection, along with another professor called Socrates. Yes, Socrates, of all people. Talk about names dropping out of context by a few millennia.

The students who were banned came to see me about their situation. I was surprised but admittedly tickled to see Denise Tate among them. It was hard to believe she had ever been a softspoken freshman hiding in the back of my class. Mark Birch's presence, on the other hand, was fairly predictable.

"Being banned isn't the end of the world," I assured them. "It's common for college students to run afoul of businesses or citizens within a stone's throw of their prospective campus. This type of stuff goes on all the time all over college towns across the United States. It's an ongoing love-hate relationship. Townies love college students as customers and cheap labor but hate them as neighbors. All you need to do is apologize and promise to behave." I leaned back in my chair and recalled an ancient memory. "I was banned once."

"You were?" Mark asked, his eyes widening.

"Yeah," I said. "While I was an undergraduate at Baker University. I got into a dispute with college officials over the allocation of land facing a strip of local businesses off campus. I petitioned for the university to allow students to gather there in lieu of getting into trouble on campus for demonstrating, signing petitions, and having radical speakers talk to students on controversial subjects."

"What kinds of subjects?"

I frowned thoughtfully. "Mostly those promoted by CORE, SNCC, and SDS, which at the time were a no-go on campus for assorted reasons. Baker was committed to staying apolitical in social and cultural matters. The university provost threw me a bone when he allowed my FSM group to populate this parcel of land just outside the south gate. The only caveat was that I had to get local businesses located on the strip nearby to support it. When I went door to door soliciting support from local businesses to create a green space for university students to meet and hold rallies, I was met with stiff resistance. The businesses weren't interested in rallies, speeches, or protests of any kind. All told, the university wanted nothing to do with politics or radicalism on campus, and local businesses didn't want students just outside the gate raising Cain. Unlike your current situation, it wasn't a local matter but something that many college students faced during the 1960s, on and off campus."

"So, what should we do?" Denise asked in a tone that betrayed frustration but also a hint of fear.

"Stay calm and advocate for your rights as patrons of local businesses. Focus on your arguments for free speech, freedom of assembly, and due process. Stay away from the Decorah townies for a week or so until I can think of how to help you resolve your issue on my end." I felt a pang of guilt for my students' current predicament. "I started all of this with my Socrates assignment and telling you to apply it to your daily lives. I'm partly responsible for what happened."

After Denise and the others left my office, I drove home, took Socrates for a walk, and then whipped up an early dinner of toasted cheese sandwiches and tomato soup. Afterward, I retired to my study to reflect on how to proceed. I was dealing with three parties: the students in question, the townies, namely the bookstore and café owners, and the powers that be at Simpson College. I could only shake my head. Only a few weeks earlier I had been trying to smooth over the Simpson student union uprising. Once again, my Socrates assignment had me skating on thin ice. Knowing full well that I was in a no-win situation and unable to resist helping my students, I did the next best thing in troubleshooting the matter: I called Hap, a world-class problem solver, if there was ever one. Well, except for the shovel and rationales about adopting stray pets that follow me home.

"You got a moment?" I asked after he picked up.

"Sure. I'm just finishing dinner. What's up?"

"I was hoping to pick your brain on something."

He was silent for a moment on the other end of the line. "I'll come over the first chance I get."

"I appreciate it," I said. "And sorry for tearing you away from your better half."

About an hour later, Hap waltzed through the front door calling for Socrates to make an appearance. "Socrates, Socrates, where art thou, Socrates?" he bellowed in his baritone. He turned to me. "You have an affinity for attracting the wrong type of attention when it comes to the other Socrates. Every time you challenge the status quo, trouble follows."

I laughed at the jab. "Did you hear the townies think one of the ringleaders of the students is Professor Socrates?"

Now Hap was the one who was laughing. "How 'bout I go downtown to the bookstore and café dressed as Professor Socrates? Somebody needs to stand up to the townies for harassing Simpson's finest."

"What would you wear?"

"Toga, white wig, and beard," he said with another hearty laugh. He took a seat on the couch in the living room and motioned for me to follow suit. "All joking aside, I don't think I need to remind you that your first duty is to the administration. You're representing the college on and off campus, whether you like it or not. To your credit, you're in good standing with Simpson, student uprising or not. But it might be a good idea to go to your department head and the dean of students and offer to deescalate the situation before it gets serious."

"What should I say?"

"Tell them that it was a teachable moment for your

students and that you'll be making a goodwill gesture on the part of the college to the townies. Once you get the green light, talk to each store owner one-on-one and in a civil tone. Say something like, 'Obviously, these young students went off half-cocked, but now they have a newfound wisdom. They know they took it a bit too far." Hap leaned in closer as he spoke. "The key is to appeal to their better nature and their business acumen. Then offer to visit other business owners who felt disrespected by these rowdy students. Remind the store owners that students like to talk to their friends, and if they don't feel welcome, downtown will lose business. It's all about the bottom line. The last thing these business owners need before the end of the semester is a costly civil war between the students and the townies."

I shook my head. "Nobody wants a civil war before school lets out. All I want is to make it to the end of the semester and start my summer vacation. Let's face it: It's just a minor fuss started by three students who happened to stand up for the right things at the wrong time."

"You're right about no need for a civil war," Hap said, laughing. "How about we settle for mounting a few police cars and giving grandiose speeches that last five minutes each and call it done? We could talk about the right to conduct commerce in the town square of our choice, to shop or not to shop as a scholar of Simpson College."

After Hap left, I lay down on the couch with a splitting headache. Socrates sat on the end of the couch, giving me a look that said, "Not again, Dad." I got him a bone from the kitchen and nodded off to sleep. Hard to believe, but his silence was just what I needed as I tried to decompress for a few hours. It was enough to put me to sleep for a spell, only to be awakened by the telephone ringing in the other room.

I stumbled into the kitchen in time to catch the call before it rang off the hook.

"Hey," a woman said in a familiar voice. "It's Norah. Just calling to check up on you. How are you?"

I waited for the cobwebs to clear before replying. "I'm doing okay. School's almost out for the summer."

She paused, clearly not convinced. "Are you sure you're okay?"

I heaved a heavy sigh and then gave her a quick recap of the latest developments.

"It sounds like a teachable moment to me," she

said after patiently listening to my story.

"That's exactly what Hap said."

"Great minds and all that," she said. "Is this something that the students can manage on their own?"

"Yeah, but my name was mentioned and with a degree of contempt."

"If you do anything on behalf of the students, will it hurt your standing with Simpson?"

I thought for a moment. "No, provided that I do it aboveboard and with the college's blessing. I need to mention it to my dean of students and make it sound like it was his idea in the first place. Obviously, the college needs its good name and to remain in the good graces of the townies. It's Community Relations 101, but it's also a generational issue. It was an older business owner who felt like someone was attacking his reputation and business. The fact that he deemed the students a necessary evil did not help the matter."

"Sounds like you have a young Turks problem to me."

It was like she could read my mind or something.

"Is time on your side?" she asked. "That is, do you have some time to put thought into a plan of attack before you act on behalf of your students?"

I nodded, still cradling the phone to my ear. "I guess so. Slow but sure was my initial thought on the matter."

"So," she said, "there you have it. Take your time— but not too much time—and get the college to back you up on any contact you make with the locals, or as you say, the 'townies.'"

"How much do I owe you for the session, Doctor?" I quipped. "It seems you've helped me resolve this problem for now."

"It's on the house," she said. "I'll get some real cash out of you later for something real important."

We laughed and bid farewell.

I hung up the phone and marveled at what had just happened. Conversations with Norah always seemed so easy—and harmonious. I felt comfortable to be witty and to engage in playful banter. Conversations with her sister Sarah, on the other hand, had degenerated into endless arguments with little or no resolution.

I had found through the years that my way of resolving things was to doodle and make lists on paper. The habit served me well when I was stressed or needed to think through things. I guess you could say it was my way of praying in a secular fashion, with little regard for asking for help from above, at least not right away. When it came to praying, deity upstairs or not, I was of the opinion that it couldn't hurt. My list-making was like chopping wood in a forest; only my ax was a pen, and the wood was the blank page. As far as the outdoors went, I had retired from it long ago. The closest I got to nature was my backyard, near the fire pit with a glass of wine.

After a few hours of back-and-forth with pen and paper and my thoughts about the townies and my students, I produced three ideas—or better yet, *steps*— to resolve my dilemma.

The first step was to write a brief note in my best penmanship to the bookstore and café owners apologizing for the recent episode and asking each of them if I could stop by for a short visit to mend fences. I would also mention how I wanted the college and its students to remain in their good graces. I noted that I would visit with my students to remind them how important it was to stay on the right side of the business owners of Decorah.

It didn't take long to write the letters. Once finished, I dropped each into an envelope, added my business card, and sealed the envelope shut.

The second step was to fashion a list of important points to go over with my students about what had happened, with the understanding that they were to take the high ground no matter what happened after I talked to the townies. As part of step two, I made a list of talking points for the townies. They were short and sweet. Anything more than four short talking points and the whole matter would go over their heads. I didn't want to lose them and let this opportunity to mend relations between them and my students slip. No matter how I looked at it, the list had to be short, to the point, and poignant. More importantly, whatever I did, said, or suggested, I would have to make it sound like it was their idea to begin with. I also made a mental note to make sure I didn't bring up Socrates, the assignment, or the missing professor so duly named.

When I finished, it was close to 11:00 p.m., and I was tired. I set down my notes on my desk, looked at Socrates, and remarked, "So how did I do?"

He stared at me, raised his eyebrows, and sighed. It was time for his evening walk, which would be followed by his doggie treat and then bedtime.

Step three entailed going around the house,

reading aloud what I had written, and committing it to memory. I not only wanted to make sure I had left nothing out; I wanted it to sound natural and authentic, as well as sincere. I had found that this practice was tried and true. I had had plenty of practice over the years doing the same thing for conference papers and seminar presentations. The last thing I wanted to do was to come off as lecturing or condescending in any way.

- - -

When I got to campus the next day, I ran into Denise Tate and Mark Birch.

"Good morning," I said. "You two will be happy to know that I'm going to talk to the townies."

Denise's face brightened. "Great!"

"Just relax and stay the course. At the end of the day, this type of stuff, where an older generation struggles to understand and relate to a younger generation on matters of social and economic justice, is as old as the hills."

The two followed as I continued to my office.

"I'm sorry again, Professor, for everything." Worry lines stretched from Mark's furrowed brow. "It all started when the bookstore owner started chewing out one of his clerks for messing up the cash drawer. The clerk is one of my fraternity brothers. He's new at the store and still learning how to ring up sales. I felt compelled to step in and set the owner straight. The store owner has forgotten that he was young once and made mistakes himself."

- - -

I met with the two store owners a week later. An angular man with a receding hairline and a somewhat stooped posture, Mr. Gallagher was sweeping the sidewalk in front of the café under a hazy sky. "I appreciate the letter," he said. "I think I might have overreacted. I should have taken the conversation to the other side of the store and hashed it out quietly. Several of my long-time customers saw the whole thing and read me the riot act afterward. That was when I realized I needed to take a step back and rethink the situation." He wiped a bead of sweat from his forehead. "Truth be told, I've been under a lot of pressure lately. The store's doing poorly, and I'm struggling to keep my clerks in line. Most of them are students at the college and have had their hours cut due to slow sales. They're not happy, but the last thing I needed was to hear from them."

Two doors down at the café, Mrs. Blanchard, the owner struck, a similar tone. "Business is slow." She nodded toward the new Starbucks store across the street. "They're some start-up from Seattle, of all places. Why can't those West Coast people leave us alone? They should sell their overpriced lattes somewhere else."

As I had with Mr. Gallagher, I mostly just listened. Mrs. Blanchard was getting on in years, her gray hair starting to fade to white, and it was clear she didn't have the energy to compete with a hip, new coffee shop.

When she was finished, I did my best to placate her. "I'll visit with my students and make the suggestion that they patronize your businesses. I'll invoke their goodwill, and if that doesn't work, I'll appeal to their small-town pride. We can't have some out-of-town shop run you out of business. Your place is an institution, and the students know that." I glanced down at the scuffed and worn checkerboard floor. "Students have been making memories here for years."

Later, as I drove home with CCR as my soundtrack, I couldn't help thinking about how lucky I was to have been able to talk to Hap and Norah and bounce ideas off them. Their ability to listen and render sound advice in the face of adversity was priceless. The last thing I needed was to get into trouble with Simpson College or, God forbid, the townies. Of course, there were still my students. I would have to save face with them and also be their advocate. Yes, advocate—the adult in the room willing to roll up his sleeves and do some dirty work on their behalf without judgment or condemnation.

18

FOR WHOM THE BELL TOLLS

"The greatest way to live with honor in this world is to be what we pretend to be."
—Socrates

As the semester drew to an end and I scored the final exams, I reflected on the year's academic events and examined my coursework and its impact on my students. I had learned a long time ago not to take course reviews and final grades to heart. You can never control those types of things. What I could control, however, were my efforts to improve the materials and how I presented them. I had found that the professors who did so were the ones the students come back to time and time again.

The uprising at the Simpson student union building had revealed what I was up against when it came to teaching philosophy at a small liberal arts college. A fair number of students considered philosophy to be a dead course offering. And to make matters worse, the Simpson administration agreed. It was not lost on me that I needed to make inroads to get the word out that philosophy was not, in fact, dead but alive and well. If I had to do some self-promotion among the student body to get those seats filled and keep the administration happy, so be it.

I walked across campus, the air ripe with spring blossoms, and found my way to my favorite bench. When I got there, I was surprised to see an envelope with a letter inside. I sat down, opened it, and started to read.

Dear Professor,

I wanted to drop you a quick line to say hello and to let you know I was thinking about what we talked about the last time we met. I visited your favorite bench a few times in hopes we could talk and I could learn more about your dear friend Socrates and his influences on the Western world. More importantly, I wanted to hear about your take on the protest in the student union. As the saying goes, there are always two sides to the story. I'm hoping we can meet up next fall and get caught up. I plan to return to Simpson next year and take your course in the fall semester. Again, nice to meet you and learn about Socrates and your take on the importance of philosophy, how it relates to the real world, and its impact on the life of a Simpson college student.

Regards,

Chad Pearson

I smiled to myself. Even though I had only met Chad once and by happenstance, I remembered the encounter fondly. It was not lost on me that my influence extended beyond the traditional classroom sometimes. It felt good to know that my teaching had inspired others, that students found it valuable and impactful, even outside my classroom.

After I put the letter in my pocket, I started to

think about my other students. Of course, the Socrates debacle still troubled me. It wasn't about what the students had read or the arguments they had made; it was how something so simple had been misunderstood and had led to a campus disturbance. In retrospect, what bothered me the most was the lack of ambition to challenge the conventional wisdom of the moment as it related to their lives on and off campus. Students didn't seem to understand the power of dissent and were unsure of their roles as active agents in shaping history.

Long and short of it all, I had survived the same thing at Baker University in the early 1960s. No longer were significant issues being mulled over, debated, and challenged. It pained me to see college students being turned into sheep, only to be led in robot fashion to their intellectual and spiritual demise. Perhaps I had become jaded. I had been in the thick of it in my youth some thirty years earlier.

Society, particularly as it related to life on campus, seemed to be in a state of retrogression of sorts. College life had been flipped over and turned inside out, which in turn had dramatically impacted the academic lives of students and professors. Gone were the days when university and college administrators had been operating under the auspices of *in loco parentis*, whereby they were responsible for being protective of and vigilant toward their charges from semester to semester.

Conversely, the college experience had turned into an exercise in getting as many students enrolled, staged, and housed on campus so the college could process their student fees and tuition on time (while they secured their generous student loans). The endeavor included dragging them back to campus each year so they could graduate in five years or less while being appropriately indoctrinated in the dutiful and faithful alumni program. Sadly, this included hitting them up for money to keep the cycle going for the next six or seven decades. Its purpose was code for, "Don't forget your alma mater in your will."

But perhaps the Socrates assignment had inspired a baby revolution. Perhaps it would serve as a small example of the social and moral drift on campuses across America. Social activism and dissent on campus now had less to do with the outside world and more to do with the goings-on on campus. Students had different priorities. They wanted better food, more social activities, improved Greek life, and a winning football team. I needed to be aware of the concerns of the modern student. By using Socrates and his words within the confines of my course, I could reach some of them with subject matter that carried a moral imperative, reinforced it, and signaled a call to duty. Even though Socrates was long gone, the spirit of his work lived on.

I owed the Greek philosopher a debt of gratitude. Yes, this gratitude also extended to Socrates, the dog I had adopted. Both of them helped me put my academic and private life into proper perspective, and lately, it seemed like things were headed in the right direction. I felt ready to bury the past, take stock of my good fortune in the present moment, and, of course, gaze toward a bright future with a new love in my life.

All told, I was one of the lucky ones who got to experience bliss in and out of the classroom each fall and spring doing something that I loved and that resonated with me. That bliss included kicking a few leaves around the quad each fall with Simpson students.

ONE LAST THING

On one of my last visits to my office before summer break, I found a small parcel waiting for me in my staff mailbox. I smiled when I spotted the return address: It was from Norah via the Chicago USPS. I opened it immediately and read the letter inside.

Dear Patrick,

I wanted to drop you a short note to say hi and to let you know I was thinking about you. More importantly, I'm writing to see if you'd be interested in taking a trip to Paris at the end of June. Yes, the one and only Paris, France. I have to finish some Chicago Art Institute requisitions and some other museum business I've been working on. Would you like to go with me? I hope so. I'll cover all the meals and hotel; you just have to cover the airfare. I promise to work really hard to have my work completed by the early afternoon each day so we can go sightseeing soon after. I have some suggestions for you if you choose to tour on your own while I'm working. I know a couple of bookstores on the Left Bank you could visit and some quiet cafés where you can read and write. Let me know soon so I can make arrangements with my Paris contacts. If you're worried about Socrates, no problem. Hap is on board to watch him while you're gone.

Au revoir!

Norah,
XOXO

At the bottom of the parcel, previously hidden under the letter, was a little statue of the Eiffel Tower. How lucky I was to have met a woman ready and able to get me out of my shell and take me on a new adventure.

Paris wasn't Athens, but it was close.

ACKNOWLEDGMENTS

Typical of most acknowledgments, the author thanks those who took the time to read multiple drafts of this manuscript and offer suggestions on how to improve it. Needless to say, this book is largely the byproduct of those efforts.

The author would also like to acknowledge the scholars who authored books that contributed greatly to providing historical facts to help drive the narrative of this book. While most of the material served as content to help move the story along, it proved invaluable nonetheless. It is in vain that this book hopes to contribute to the genre of historical fiction.

ABOUT THE AUTHOR

The author is a former US Marine and post-secondary educator turned novelist. He holds several advanced degrees related to the study of the humanities and has published several articles and coauthored academic anthologies. These scholarly pursuits have afforded him the opportunity to travel to more than thirteen different countries. His historical interests include World War I, the Cold War, and the counterculture of the 1960s.

He now lives in Denton, Texas.